Praise f‌ ‌ Days

"A strange and marvelously ve
is intelligently conceive gly
original. A compelling p 1ul cal
vitality."

—*Kirkus Reviews*

"What begins as a science fiction hoax becomes a psychological thriller, a double hitter that packs a painful punch."

—*Midwest Book Review*

"The dramatic tension of *Black Days* is perfect throughout. Nobody is going to put this book down."

—**Howard Frank Mosher,** author of
Where the Rivers Flow North, Disappearances

"Jackson Ellis has come up with a most unusual marriage of fairly straight literary realism and over-the-top phantasmagoria that is the more successful for its quiet, understated narration. It's fast-paced, compelling, and equipped with a hero-narrator whom the reader likes and sympathizes with from the outset."

—**Castle Freeman, Jr.**, author of *Go With Me,*
The Devil in the Valley

"Jackson Ellis combines the subtlety of a Don DeLillo with the fearlessness of Stephen King. If you love stories that take you on a wild ride from introspective narrative to sinister revelation you'll enjoy *Black Days*. You'll never predict what the next turn in the horrifying journey will be until you take the trip."

—**Bill Morgan,** author of *I Celebrate Myself,*
The Typewriter Is Holy

Praise for *Lords of St. Thomas*

"*Lords of St. Thomas* masterfully couples a historic event with a classic coming-of-age story . . . [offering] a glimpse into the past and a glimmer of hope for the future."

—*Midwest Book Review*

"Beautifully written, *Lords of St. Thomas* is the story of tragedies leading to subsequent tragedies [and] a thoughtful portrayal of the human consequences of major environmental changes."

—*Historical Novel Society*

"A thrilling story where readers measure how much they value their rights and how far they're willing to fight for them . . . Ellis does a compelling job of showing the Lord family's nearly noble hopelessness in their fight to change a fait accompli, without capitulating to sentimentality. This tragic note gives a particular, Steinbeckian vividness to the familiar templates of multigenerational family tale (the story of the Lords) and the American coming-of-age narrative (the story of Little Henry)."

—*New England Review of Books*

"A sparsely eloquent, elegiac novel."

—*Seven Days*

"A great story and one that I found hard to put down, reading it from cover to cover during a quiet rainy evening. Ellis vividly evokes place and person in a style that Mosher himself admired."

—*Manchester Journal*

"*Lords of St. Thomas* is a timely, tender, thought-provoking family saga about the importance of keeping promises—no matter how long they take to fulfill. With a playful touch, Jackson Ellis has gifted us with a daring story rich in premise and intrigue with just the right amount of suspense and pathos."

—**Nathaniel G. Moore**, author of *Jettison*

"With *Lords of St. Thomas,* Jackson Ellis has written a book that is part historic, part environmental, part familial, and always compelling. Ellis draws us deep into the lives of the Lord family as they face the loss of their home, their community, their way of life, and even themselves to the rising waters of Lake Mead. And we readers are sucked along as the family wrestles with the decision to leave or stay while fighting to survive. It's a story that forces the reader to keep reading, one page after the next, to see what becomes of historic St. Thomas—and what becomes of the Lords."

—**Sean Prentiss**, author of *Finding Abbey: The Search for Edward Abbey and His Hidden Desert Grave*

BLACK
DAYS

Also by Jackson Ellis

Lords of St. Thomas

BLACK DAYS

a novel

Jackson Ellis

GREEN WRITERS PRESS *Brattleboro, Vermont*

Printed in the United States

10 9 8 7 6 5 4 3 2

Green Writers Press is a Vermont-based publisher whose mission
is to spread a message of hope and renewal through the words and
images we publish. Throughout we will adhere to our commitment to
preserving and protecting the natural resources of the earth. To that
end, a percentage of our proceeds will be donated to environmental
activist groups. Green Writers Press gratefully acknowledges support
from individual donors, friends, and readers to help support the
environment and our publishing initiative.

Giving Voice to Writers & Artists Who Will Make the World a Better Place
Green Writers Press | Brattleboro, Vermont • www.greenwriterspress.com

ISBN: 979-8-9891784-5-2

Cover art and design by Nathaniel Pollard | hello@nathanpollard.com

PRINTED ON PAPER WITH PULP THAT COMES FROM FSC-CERTIFIED FORESTS, MANAGED FORESTS THAT
GUARANTEE RESPONSIBLE ENVIRONMENTAL, SOCIAL, AND ECONOMIC PRACTICES. ALL WOOD
PRODUCT COMPONENTS USED IN BLACK & WHITE, STANDARD COLOR, OR SELECT COLOR
PAPERBACK BOOKS, UTILIZING EITHER CREAM OR WHITE BOOKBLOCK PAPER
ARE SUSTAINABLE FORESTRY INITIATIVE® (SFI®) CERTIFIED SOURCING.

When night gets started, it just won't stop.

—RICHARD BRAUTIGAN

PART
I

1.

My father was pushing forty when his mom died. I was only twelve. It was the first time either of us had witnessed the death of another person, and we shared the experience on a sunny and otherwise pleasant Sunday afternoon, shortly after lunchtime, in the summer of 1943. It hit both of us hard. It might have been even harder for him. It was his mother, after all, and when you're middle aged, as he was, the reality of your own impending death starts to creep up on you.

In a way, the death of another is a preview of your own. And the passing of your parents means you've stepped up. You're next in line.

About a month before, a heart attack downed Grandma in the kitchen like a hatchet fells timber in the forest, hard and swift. Pneumonia is what finally did her in, slowly and patiently. I watched her go, a death rattle fading in her throat as she stared glassy-eyed at the ceiling above the twin brass bed in the room next to mine. Then she exhaled her final thin, wheezy breath, and the light in her eyes, flickering like a candle flame in a gentle breeze, snuffed itself out. If thin ribbons of smoke had drifted from her pupils just then I would not have been surprised. I froze, staring at the clouds gathering in her corneas.

Weeping and trembling, my mother closed my grandma's eyes with two gentle fingertips, and then placed a heavy silver dollar over each eyelid to hold them shut. I thought it was strange how she had the silver dollars handy in her pocket. She'd obviously been holding onto them for a while, saving them for this exact moment. Sometimes in town she'd surprise me with money for a chocolate bar or a root beer. Now she surprised me with money intended for my dead grandmother's face.

Though it had been peaceful, the death and all its aftermath was practically unbearable to witness. But I toughed it out, and I stayed at the bedside to share in the shuddering sobs of my parents. For a few days, I thought the tears would never stop flowing. But of course, within the week, blubbery anguish was supplanted by an air of quiet, tacit melancholy that lingered in our home like thick fog.

The following weekend, my dad and I found ourselves dry-eyed and silent, leaning against the railing of the wooden bridge that crossed the Mad River, just down the road from our century-old, whitewashed Vermont farmhouse. Dad and I had come to hook a few trout, but in the daze of my despair, I'd left our tackle box on the porch. So we stood there, staring, thinking, each foolishly clutching a fishing rod we couldn't use.

Finally he broke the silence.

"Death dies with death," he pronounced, slowly and thoughtfully. He looked into the water in search of further words. "What I mean is, when you die, the *idea* of death dies with you. And so the *fear* of death only dies when you die, because only when you die does death cease to exist. Am I making any sense? I mean, do you understand what I'm trying to say?"

He paused for only a second, giving me no time to form a response to the odd statement.

"Well? Do you?"

"I think so," I replied, not really understanding his point, nor particularly caring. I was too sad to care.

"No," he said, not falling for my pat response. "You don't. Listen. You can only be afraid of things if you know they exist. Right? If you don't know something exists, you can't be afraid of it."

"But everyone knows what it means to be dead," I argued half-heartedly, swatting at mosquitoes.

"Nobody knows what it's *like* to be dead. Sure, we can come up with abstract ideas of what it's *like* to die and be dead. But we don't really understand it, so we're afraid of it. But dead people...they don't know anything. Dead people don't have ideas or fears. That's the wonderful thing about being dead. You no longer feel afraid."

Grandma hadn't looked afraid, I thought. Disappointed, but not afraid. When we were alone she told me as much:

"I'm so sorry I won't be around to watch you grow up, Daniel." That was one of the last things she said to me. Near-death frailty hadn't softened any of the anger in her weak, breathy voice.

"I'm not afraid of it," I replied to my father.

"You're young yet," Dad countered. "Someday, the fear will get you. It'll sneak up and grab you from behind when you least expect it, and it will never let you go. People come and go in your life, but when you see your parents go, it *really* gets you. Suddenly, you realize, your own time is coming." He stopped his rambling and paused. Then he sighed. "I wasn't afraid of anything when I was young. Now, I sure am."

He sniffed. "I shouldn't be saying all of this to you. Come on. Let's go get the tackle box."

I was young. At the time, I couldn't quite understand what he was trying to express, but his words stuck with me. The older I got, the more I reflected on them, and the more afraid I became myself. Fear of death is the only true, primal fear any human being can have, and when it finally takes root, it crawls through your subconscious mind like a grapevine, and it clings to you for your entire life. You have no choice but to live with it until it dies along with you. It was a morbid, smart insight by my father.

◉

But he was wrong. My fear of death died on the dark night I nearly kicked the bucket myself, right there in the very same Mad River.

It was Christmas Eve, 1992. I'd worked a late shift at the plant. With the mortgage on the new cottage in Key Largo on my mind, I was eager to earn the double-overtime pay. In three months I'd be retired—so I'd better take the extra cash while I could still get it.

Had I gone home at my usual 5:30 quitting time, the light mist that had fallen during the day would not have yet completely frozen. But by 11:30, the mercury had plunged far below freezing, and an invisible glaze of black ice formed atop the asphalt along Route 100.

What I know of the accident is probably based less on my actual memory of it than on newspaper articles, medical reports, and what people told me in the aftermath. But who's to say? My brains haven't been right since that night years ago.

I was about halfway home, coasting along a level straightaway beside the river. CCR was playing in the tape deck, and I was sipping lukewarm decaf from a coffee-stained plastic travel mug. Before I realized what was happening, the rear tires of my 1985 Ford Ranger suddenly began to fishtail. I hadn't been turning, braking, or accelerating. The rubber simply lost the road.

Rather than panicking, I simply thought, *How odd.* A moment ago I'd been in control of the vehicle, humming along to "Proud Mary" for the millionth time and hoping that my son, home for the holidays, had left a plate of dinner for me in the microwave before heading to his mom's house. But now, my truck pirouetted as smoothly as a figure skater, and I hurtled backward toward the guardrail as my high beams illuminated the skeletal arms of the bare birches I'd just passed by. That is perhaps my most vivid visual memory: those glowing, bone-white branches.

Boom!

My face smashed into the steering wheel, crushing my forehead and nose, and then my skull ricocheted back into the headrest. The scrape and whine of metal on metal rang out from under my feet as the truck skidded up and over the slick aluminum guardrail. The rail skinned the undercarriage of the vehicle like a filleting knife paring the scales off a freshwater catch. And then the truck was flipped back, tossed into the shallow, slow-flowing Mad River.

In a wreck—in a really *bad* car wreck—you lose all sense of what is up and what is down. I mean, it's hard to understand in which direction gravity wants to pull you when you're rolling ass over teakettle, coffee cups and cassette tapes and crumpled napkins and dirt clods bouncing around like lotto balls.

After hurtling over the bank for what seemed an eternity, the truck dropped into the brook with an enormous *splash*. Dark, frigid water hissed and spurted as it threaded between expanding cracks in the passenger window. Then, seconds later, the fragile pane shattered, and an explosion of river water gushed into the cab. The truck had landed upside down; that I could tell by the way the torrent of ice and shards of glass touched my scalp first and promptly moved down my forehead, over my clenched eyes, and into my nostrils.

I swallowed a mouthful of air; then I slowly exhaled. Bubbles tickled my chin and crawled spiderlike down my neck. It hit me that my head and shoulders were now submerged in the freezing current, and I'd just taken my last dry breath. Every nerve-ending in the skin that encased my skull and throat sizzled and prickled in the ice bath.

But it was terror that sent shivers down my spine.

◉

So this is how it ends, suspended upside down in blackness and silence and swirling liquid. Like a frozen fetus. Going out the way I came in, eh? Shivering and feeble and dumb. Maybe I can reach the seatbelt buckle—shit, my arm is trapped. Must be the steering wheel pinning it down. Damn seatbelt. Things probably cost more lives than they save. God damn it, what a drag. I wish my kids were with me. No, not that. Want to see them again, though. Maybe I can find a straw and breathe through it. Do I have a straw in here? Shit, I forgot, my arm's trapped. When do I ever use a straw anyway? No, I wouldn't have a straw. Jesus, my lungs hurt. So cold. And I need air. Fuck, this is bad. This is really bad! I can't hold on anymore—I need air, I have to breathe, I HAVE TO BREATHE—

My body filled with snow. That's what it felt like. Not just my lungs and sinus cavity, but my whole head—my muscles, bones, and flesh swelled with ice water as I sucked it in through my yawning, oxygen-hungry maw. It flowed beneath my fingernails and between my fluttering, floating ribs and numbed my pounding heart. The river coursed around me and through me as if I were a sponge, soaking it all in.

It felt *wrong*. Drowning didn't hurt so much as it simply felt *wrong*. Liquid does not belong in the lungs. *Get it out*, my lungs cried. *Get it out!* What could I do though? Cough it up?

I began to cough. It was more like a spasm. Now it began to hurt. Badly.

I suffered an eternity in a matter of passing seconds, counting off heartbeats that each passed as slowly as the past decades of my life. I twisted and thrashed while the seatbelt tightened its grip on my torso the way a boa constrictor strangles its helpless prey.

Helpless! So completely helpless! A newborn left to wolves would have more of a chance of survival than a seatbelt-lashed old man flopping around like an ice fisherman's worm.

Suddenly, the pain and suffering stopped in a glorious instant, as if a switch had been flipped. Euphoric warmth spread through me like melted butter. Warmth, peace, and pure, light happiness swallowed whole my agony and fear. I stopped twitching, stopped panicking. It was sublime.

I didn't care if I died. If this is how it felt to die, I wanted to die for all eternity—not *be* dead, necessarily, but to actively *die* so that I could always feel this way. I laughed—or, at least, I seemed to laugh. Maybe I laughed in a dream. I felt my weight shifting, the sensation of spinning, tumbling, falling. Slowly, slowly I faded away into deep sleep and a darkness deeper and blacker than any I'd ever known.

Then there was nothing.

2.

Twenty minutes. That's how long they estimated I was underwater, breathless and unconscious, before I was dragged out of the river by a passing motorist.

Thankfully, the headlights of my truck stayed on and were easily seen from the road. The young ski tourist from Connecticut who saved my life, yet whose name I never found out, leaped from his car, waded into the water, and somehow pulled me from the tangled seatbelt and dragged me to shore. He stayed with me on the riverbank just below the road—surely freezing himself, with soaked pants and shoes—while his wife drove to the nearest house to call for help.

Shortly thereafter, an ambulance showed up and I was strapped to a stretcher for the long drive to the nearest emergency room. My anonymous saviors, to whom I owe my life, went on their way like nameless ghosts. Hopefully they enjoyed a lovely holiday vacation free from further brushes with drowning old fools.

Despite my being as limp and lifeless as a wet noodle, a pair of paramedics beat the water from my lungs and put the paddles to my chest—and sure enough, on a frost-heaved stretch of road somewhere between the crash site and the hospital in Rutland, I was raised from the dead like Saint Lazarus.

In a medical sense, that is what happened: I was *clinically* dead, my truck wreck discovered after I'd gone into cardiac arrest—and *long* after I had stopped breathing. In fact, I likely went a half-hour without taking a single breath.

Had I endured the same accident in, say, mid-June or even in mid-October, I wouldn't be here today to tell you about it. I'd have drowned within a few minutes.

The doctors who treated me explained it like this: In near-freezing water, the body rapidly enters hypothermia. While only my head and part of my torso were underwater, the MDs confirmed that the partial bodily submersion plus the effect of the amount of water I inhaled was sufficient to cause me to become hypothermic, slowing my heartbeat and preserving oxygen already stored in my body—a supreme blessing when you can't breathe.

Hypothermia has two other benefits that served me well. First, in its quest for self-preservation, the hypothermic body directs the slowed flow of blood to organs that need it most, namely the heart and brain. And secondly, perhaps more importantly, extreme cold reduces the amount of oxygen required by the brain, allowing it to survive free of substantial damage for surprisingly long, airless periods of time.

Again, had it been spring, summer, or fall, I would have drowned immediately. Instead, I was essentially frozen alive, preserved just long enough to be resuscitated. I escaped with my life and suffered only mild hypoxic injury.

In other words, I cheated death.

Unfortunately, after a brief couple of waking minutes in the hospital, I succumbed to a four-month coma. I remember nothing of it. Christmas, New Year's Day, multiple snowstorms, the vernal equinox, opening day at Fenway Park, and the blooming of spring's first flowers and leaf buds occurred while I lay comatose, eating through a stomach tube and pissing out a catheter.

I also slept through my sixty-second birthday and my final months of employment. I didn't come to until weeks after what should have been my big retirement send-off.

It wouldn't be a celebration I'd awaken to, but rather a waking nightmare—a continuation of the one I'd been living for thirteen years.

3.

Growing older is strange. One day, you hop out of bed with the same energy you had when you were 18. Your body feels good, and your mind feels better. You haven't lost an ounce of vigor over the decades, you're sure of it.

The day passes along. At some point, you catch a glimpse of a reflection of an old man in a car window or in a puddle. He looks like one of many, many men you might've seen years ago when growing to such an age yourself seemed as inconceivable as winning the lottery or visiting Mars.

But it's you. You're still straggling along with a light bank account. You never made it to Mars, nor to most of the more plausible destinations you'd wished to visit. But you certainly grew old. Seeing your withering features reminds you that no matter how good you feel today, tomorrow could easily be a different story—and that age, after all, *isn't* just a state of mind.

Aging might be more pleasant, to some extent, if shared with a partner to whom you grow closer and more in love as you inch closer to your last sunset. But I divorced fairly young and never remarried. Having so much solitude gives you a lot of time to think, and when you have ample time to think, you end up dwelling on the past. I don't know why, but it's never the good things you focus on.

I spent years using hard work and various hobbies to smother my regrets and mistakes, only to have them bubble up to the surface and consume me as I approached retirement age. In a way, it makes sense. When you are young, your life is an unwritten book, full of promise. When you are old, you've nearly completed your story, and it can never be edited, altered, or erased. So much remains undone. Then the back cover closes.

My story had been neither a fairytale nor a tragedy, though it resembled both at various times. First the former, then the latter.

Right out of high school, my girlfriend, Sandy, went off to college in southern Connecticut. Though I'd graduated alongside her with fine grades myself, I wasn't quite ready to go back to school right away. So I stayed behind in my hometown of Granbury, Vermont, answering the call for a temporary laborer at the cheese factory down the road in Belfield. The money was great: ninety-five cents an hour weighing, traying, and packaging cheddar wheels. The plan was that I'd work for a while, save up money, and then take a forestry course. By the time she finished her education, Sandy would be qualified to get a job as a dental assistant, and then we could move west to Montana or Oregon like we'd planned for years.

Then, in 1952, she got pregnant. We exchanged wedding vows shortly thereafter, in early November, and our daughter Mary arrived in June of 1953. We were both barely twenty-two years old.

Suddenly, the cheese job wasn't so much a temporary position as a permanent, full-time station. In 1962, I took up additional work as a part-time line technician at the brand new plastics manufacturing plant, Murphy Industries, over in Brookton. After a few years of working days at the cheese factory and nights as a production line wage slave, I became full-time and salaried at Murphy's, receiving on-the-job training to become a well-paid supervisor. With a twelve-year-old daughter and a toddler son now at home, I couldn't possibly turn it down. It wouldn't be forever—in fact, it would help us quickly pay for the home we'd bought on Old Stage Road, not even a mile from the house I grew up in. We planned to hang around—just for a few more years.

"A few more years." It's what you tell yourself when you're already sunk in the mud with spinning wheels. See, when you are in the middle of it, you don't realize that life and its myriad opportunities are slipping by. You keep waiting and dreaming, always believing there is a finish line to cross *just* beyond the horizon, where your struggles will conclude. Soon you will have enough money and time—you can feel it. When that time comes, you can put your plans into action.

Forestry in Montana or Oregon—or, hell, maybe deep-sea fishing off the southeastern coast of Florida. I could send the kids to high school in the Keys. It was my future—*our* future—and it was bright.

We raised two great kids, all the while losing track of time in the years of "Gootchy-goo!" and "Loop, swoop, and pull," and "Catch the ball with two hands!" and "I'm not sure what *x* equals. Ask your mother." Fortunately for us, by the time they were both out of the house, Sandy and I were relatively young yet. It was time to move on and live the good life we'd dreamed of long ago.

◎

I came home from work on a Tuesday evening in May of 1980 to find my wife sitting on the living room couch, waiting for me. Dried, encrusted tears and mascara made stripes across her swollen, puffy cheeks, and her clasped hands rested in her lap atop an old flower-printed cotton dress. She looked exhausted, with red, bloodshot eyes. She'd been crying for hours, it was clear to see, so I dropped to my knees beside her and took her hand in mine, my heart pounding as I waited to hear the name of the person who had died.

"What is it?" I asked softly. "What happened?"

She could barely look at me. We made eye contact for a brief moment before she looked away and shielded her eyes with her free hand. Suddenly, I had an epiphany:

This was not a woman in mourning. I knew her well enough to recognize grief—together, we'd been through the losses of her father, both of my parents, four grandparents, two dogs, and nearly a half-dozen cats. No. It was guilt that had overtaken her—I could see it, and it made me even more anxious. So much so that I nearly stood up and walked out of the room before she could speak. Maybe if I left, we could pretend this had never happened, and she could forever hang onto the words she was about to say.

But I stayed; I took a deep breath and she did the same. Irritably, her hand fell to her lap and she looked up and off to the side, as if in search of a script written on the ceiling. She exhaled another long sigh through pursed lips. Then she jumped into it, sprinting into her prepared remarks and spitting words at full-speed, afraid they'd never come otherwise.

"I love you, Daniel, but I don't—I'm not—I'm not *in love* anymore. I don't think I can do this anymore. I can't."

I knew those words, or similar words, were coming, but there was no way to brace for them. It was like a hard sledge had been dropped on my heart.

Not in love? Not with me? To be sure, after decades together, the passion might have faded. But the *love*? It was stronger than ever, I'd thought. We were finally a couple again, without children in the house, on the threshold of embarking on the long-delayed adventures we'd planned together.

Placidly, I dropped her hand, stood up, and looked away from her in sudden disgust. I began to pace around the room, remaining silent, allowing her to continue.

"I feel like—I think—we've had a great life together. It was just wonderful for so long, and we raised such wonderful kids. You're a wonderful father—"

"Sounds like a pretty *wonderful* thing we had," I snapped. "Just not *wonderful* enough for such a *wonderful* woman." My sudden nasty tone gave her ample reason to be defensive and play the victim, and just enough ammunition to double-down on her offense.

"Don't be like that. See? You're always so quick to snap at me! Do you really think it's pleasant being around you all the time? Do you think you're pleasant to be with? With your moods, and your—your . . . *attitude?*"

The question hung in the air as I regarded her with a blank expression. She waited for me to fill the vacuum, but I refused. Standing there, so close to her but feeling oceans of distance between us, I was filled with anger and hate directed in equal shares at us both. Concurrent desires to shake sense into her, strike her, and smother her in love came in waves accompanied by mild nausea, and knowing that none were actions that would make any difference made me feel helpless. Suddenly I had regret— my first true, crushing feelings of regret in my life, where I knew that my chances, if any, to fix this situation had long since passed. I'd lost her completely before I even realized I'd been losing her all along.

Her face relaxed and unknotted as if she were struck with a sudden bolt of guilt. She'd wanted to let me down easily, but had attacked at the slightest provocation. Switching gears and changing her tune, my soon-to-be-ex-wife cooed, "I love you, I really do, but I just don't feel close to you anymore. But I will always care about you."

A pause. An expectant, hopeful look on her face. I said nothing.

"I think you deserve better than this," she continued to prattle. "You deserve someone better than me, who can love you with her whole heart and not just go through the motions. I'm doing this because I love you too much to hurt you—to lie to you. I hope this doesn't ruin things between us." She began to cry again.

"How long have you felt like this?" I asked in a monotone voice.

She hung her head. "A long time." Then she repeated it. "A long time."

"Is there someone else?"

"No! No, no," she wailed. "I could never do that to you—no, no. I just need to be alone!"

Alone? Other than weekends and five minutes in the morning before work and for an hour or two at night, we never see each other! I am always alone!

Countless words and speeches ran through my mind: declarations of love that might win her back; poisonous barbs that I hoped would knock her harder and drop her lower and cut her more deeply than anything she'd said or could possibly say or do to me. I wanted her back; simultaneously, I wanted the upper hand, and I wanted to gain it with maximum hurt.

I knew I could have neither. We'd exchanged few words, but I knew absolutely that she was a lost cause, and I had nothing to gain. I began to feel the swift onslaught of exhaustion and deep sadness, so I quipped, "Well, I'm going out for cigarettes."

"What?" she said, perplexed, snuffling back tears, thinking that perhaps I too had long held fast to a secret. "You smoke?"

"No, I don't. But I'm still going out for cigarettes." Blinking back tears, I grabbed a change of clothes from our bedroom and a banana from the kitchen.

"Don't hate me," I heard her call as I stormed out of the house. "I hope we can still treat each other—" I slammed the screen door over her last words. When I made it to my truck, I realized I'd forgotten a toothbrush and toothpaste, but decided I'd rather just buy some from the drugstore in town.

Several days later, after four nights spent in a cheap motor inn near the ski resorts, I returned home. Sandy was gone. Most of our belongings were still there. She took only what she needed to survive in her new home, wherever that might be.

I walked through the silent, creaking wooden house, feeling haunted. My ex-wife and two children still lived, but their ghosts drifted about the rooms and wandered the halls just the same.

◉

Sandy hadn't lied. There wasn't another man and, as far as I know, she never remarried. In fact, using funds from my hefty monthly alimony payments, she eventually purchased the ranch house across the road from me. The previous owner had kept horses, so other than the adjacent two-level barn long since fallen into disuse and disrepair, no other buildings existed on the five-acre lot. Just open meadows. This was in stark contrast to my home, which sat amid a shady grove of spruce and pine.

So that was it. At the top of a hill, separated by a narrow dirt road and two wide front lawns, two houses faced each other. One bathed in light, one nestled in darkness. One a symbol of a halfhearted fresh start, one full of wistful memories and hurt. She was little more than an arm's length away, but that was enough distance for her. At least, I thought, this will make it easy for the kids when they come to visit. Maybe that's why she moved back. Maybe she just missed the hilltop where she'd helped to raise our children. I don't know; we seldom conversed, and I never asked about it.

Many mornings, just before the sun began its slow rise over the hillside behind my house, I would sit in the breakfast nook, sipping black coffee in the dark. I could see Sandy's bedside light flicker on behind the drawn curtain of an upstairs window as she arose for the day. An early riser, just like me. Then the light would come on in her kitchen, and I could see her silhouette as she shuffled around, waiting for the coffee to percolate. Then she'd take a seat at her own dining table and would welcome the morning alone, like me.

And I would think, *Somehow, I guess it's better this way.*

4.

As I crawled through my final working years toward retirement, I began to lament my lot in life severely. I regurgitated regrets and mistakes and chewed them over on a nightly basis while staring at the television or lying awake in bed, eyes glued to the ceiling. Having my best years well behind me while my ex-wife sat so close by, just out of reach, was killing me. Years of waiting and dreaming had gotten me nowhere.

But around my sixtieth birthday, on a whim, I reviewed the boilerplate text of my company pension plan and received a pleasant surprise: Providing you'd worked for at least thirty years, employees of Murphy Industries could receive full retirement benefits at age sixty-two. For whatever reason, I'd long believed the retirement age to be sixty-five.

It felt like a gift from a benevolent God. Three years of my life were being returned—and with a full pension, no less.

Finally! Good fortune had come my way at last, and though I wasn't instantly gratified, *the future* was in clear sight. Five years felt like a long time. But two years? Sometimes it felt as though I sneezed and two years had passed.

I felt happy. I made plans. Big plans. My aging body was no longer interested in heading out West, so southward bound I would be. I still hadn't visited the Florida Keys, but in just two years I'd have the perfect opportunity to rent a nice seaside bungalow and pass a few winter weeks fishing, floating, and bathing in the sun like an overripe orange. Perhaps I could give Sandy a few dollars to shovel out my walk while I was gone!

Of course, she'd never take me up on something so insulting. And besides, after years of alimony, I was finally free of financial obligations to her—no need to risk becoming a debtor again. The few years since I'd cut my last check to her had certainly been kind to my bank account, as I lived simply and owed little to anyone but the utility and insurance companies. Hell, I probably could have afforded a new house if I'd wanted one . . . .

A new house. That's not a bad idea at all. Why should I merely go on vacation to the Keys? Why not finally make a clean break with this home, this town—with this state?

In no time, the decision was made. I'd move. I'd start searching for a new home as soon as I approached my final six months on the job.

◉

It didn't matter that I'd never been to Key Largo, nor laid eyes on Buttonwood Sound. The photos in the brochures that I received from the real estate company provided all I needed, ample evidence that it was exactly where I wanted to be.

In October of 1992, just two months before my accident, I placed a down payment on a small cottage a hundred yards from the water. A gorgeous, fifty-year-old white bungalow set in a private cluster of palms and whispering sawgrass, it had everything I could possibly desire: two bedrooms (one for me, one for anyone who wanted to visit), a small, sandy front yard, beach rights on the nearby sound, and even a fishing pier to launch a dinghy from. A rope hammock could be seen in one of the photos, hanging comfortably between a pair of tall thatch palms. I could see myself in it, dozing with a half-read book splayed across my chest and a tropical breeze rustling my hair.

With a price tag over a hundred and twenty thousand dollars, it was by far the costliest thing I'd ever agreed to purchase. However, I calculated that with my savings and pension combined with the money I'd get if I sold the house on Old Stage Road, I'd have just enough to survive on and still afford the mortgage. I put down a large down payment. In fact, I practically broke out in a sweat as I signed off on it. To me, it was a massive amount of money.

Despite the bittersweet memories and years spent within its walls pining for an escape, it would be hard to part with my Vermont home. Nevertheless, it was an idea I embraced, especially knowing I could stay with my daughter whenever I wished. Mary and her husband Nathaniel lived quite close by with their daughter, Elsie, right there in Granbury. They were busy people, and I saw them only when their hectic schedules allowed. But if I were forced to stay with them whenever in Vermont, it would give me more of an opportunity to actually *visit* with them. Maybe I'd get to know them a little better.

Providing a place to stay wouldn't be the first favor Mary would do for her old man. While I was in a coma, she and her husband maintained my house, keeping it ready for my hopeful return. They also deposited my final paychecks (which the company graciously paid in full) and the first of my pension checks, and paid all my bills, including the hefty payments for the Key Largo house.

When I awoke from the coma on May 5, 1993, I was told that I'd have a long road to recovery. Months, in fact.

"Will I be healthy enough for travel by wintertime?" I asked nervously.

"Oh, absolutely," said the doctor. "If you stay on track with your therapy, we expect that you'll make a full recovery by fall."

I smiled, relieved. The months had slipped by me unnoticed, and I'd passed through them in a big, empty void, a plane of existence separate from everyone else. So when I came to, my conscious mind was still as fixated on Florida as it had been the very night I'd landed upside down in my truck in the Mad River.

Yes, I'd be heading to Key Largo after all. Nothing had changed in my life. In fact, I'd gotten a nice little "vacation," four-plus months of hibernation through the long, cold Vermont winter and my last few months of work. Actually, things seemed to work out in my favor.

That's what I told myself, and that's what I chose to believe. Then, during the first week of June, I finally saw my pension check with my own eyes.

5.

I'd been home for about nine or ten days when I limped out to the mailbox at the end of the stone walkway that cut through the dooryard. Nothing but junk mail, catalogs . . . and an official-looking business envelope from Murphy Industries.

A pension check! My meal ticket, my gravy train, the fruit of my decades of labor. It wasn't my first—Mary had deposited the first couple months' worth of checks—but it would be the first one I would pull out of the envelope and deposit myself. It was the start of a biweekly ritual I was sure to enjoy.

I hobbled back into the house and slapped the pile of mail down on the dining table. In one motion, while slumping into my chair, I slid a finger into the edge of the envelope and ripped it open. Then I pulled the check out and took a look at it.

$274.28.

That certainly doesn't seem right, I thought. *They must have sent me the wrong check.*

No, right there, "Daniel Fassett," I confirmed. *There it is. It's for me.*

What the hell is going on?

The check trembled between my pinched forefinger and thumb, and I looked away and studied the porcelain plate clock hanging over the kitchen sink. Perhaps when I looked back at the check the numbers would be correct. Maybe it was just a mistake on my part.

Nope. Still only two hundred seventy-four dollars and change.

The kitchen table was where I usually sat to cut checks and pay my bills, so a calculator was always handy—just behind the salt and pepper shakers, next to Sandy's old sunflower-patterned napkin holder. I grabbed it and started to punch in numbers.

My paycheck had been about $571 a week . . . Okay, now, my pension pays out sixty percent of my final salary, putting me at—let's see . . . about $342.

They'd shorted me by almost seventy dollars! There must be, I said to myself, a reasonable explanation for this. A clerical error that needs clarifying.

I'll give HR a ring, let them know to adjust my future paychecks. Plus they can send me some extra *money to make up for the last few pension checks that they short-changed me on.*

You don't work for years on a factory floor without learning to keep your emotions in check. Panicking in a bad situation never does anyone any good. Still, as I stuck my finger into the rotary phone and began to dial up human resources, my heart pounded, and the acid in my stomach bubbled up into the back of my throat.

◉

The phone rang only once.

"Hello, Murphy Indust—"

"Hey, Sally, it's Dan."

"Daniel!" she exclaimed, genuinely happy to hear my voice. "How good to hear from you! So happy you're okay! How are you? Are you feeling better?"

"Oh, thank you, Sally, I'm feeling wonderful. I feel a little better every day." For fifteen years, I'd maintained a superficial friendship with Sally, the attractive red-headed director of human resources. Our rapport never extended beyond our office walls, but still, we respected and genuinely liked each other, and I knew she'd help me out. Though I wanted to be polite and chat, as we'd not spoken since before the accident, I couldn't have been more eager to get to the bottom of my dilemma.

"Listen, Sally," I blurted, "I hate to ask, but—"

"So are you walking already?" she cut in. "What did the doctors say? And when are you coming to visit us down here again? Everyone would *love* to see you!"

"Oh, I plan to come down real soon, yeah. Soon as I can. I'm walking just fine these days—a little slow, you know, as can be expected. Doctors say I'll recover fully. Not too much brain damage. But there's not much to damage, right?" It was a little attempt on my part at dry, self-deprecating humor, but it came out sounding flat and depressing, and I winced as I spoke the words.

But Sally cracked up as though I'd made the cleverest joke she'd ever heard. She was truly glad to hear from me.

"Ah, Daniel, we've missed you so much around here!" she gushed. "So, tell me, what was it like waking up after being in a—"

"Sally, I'm really sorry, but I have something I really need to talk to you about." It was my turn to cut her off, and I hoped she wouldn't be hurt by it. "You know the pension checks I'm supposed to be receiving?"

"*Supposed* to be?" she answered. "You mean you're not getting them? I'll look into this right away for you."

"No, no, it's not that. I'm getting them. Problem is, it's not the right amount. It's *way* less than it should be."

I continued to explain to her how much money I was receiving, and how much I was actually due. I could hear her fingertips clacking away on a calculator as she mumbled to herself, double-checking my math. Sure enough, she produced the same results: I was owed three hundred forty-two dollars and change per check.

"I don't know what to tell you, Daniel," Sally said, sharing in the frustration. "I think you'll need to speak with Mr. Thompson about this. I'll be glad to help set up a meeting with him for you. He could probably see you tomorrow afternoon."

"Thanks, but I'd rather give him a ring. I'll try him first thing in the morning—I know he's at his desk then. Thanks a lot for all your help," I said, and hung up.

John Thompson was the president of the company and had been at the helm through most of my tenure. Despite working below him, we maintained a surprisingly comfortable relationship—largely because he stayed out of my way, and I stayed out of his hair. Perhaps it was because I'd been with the company longer than him that he let me do my job free of nitpicking and micromanaging.

But the respect he showed me was an anomaly, and on a personal level, I didn't care much for the guy. I didn't like the arrogant way he talked down to most of the lower-level employees. Hell, I didn't care for the way he spoke to his own wife when I'd see them together at the annual company Christmas party. The role of "boss" was something he took seriously, and it wasn't a mere persona he adopted between eight a.m. and quitting time—it was a lifestyle evident in his gait, his dress, and his tone of voice, and he reeked of pretentiousness. Simply put, if he viewed you as less than his equal in stature, then he spoke to you as such, in a subtly condescending and sarcastic tone.

I'd stayed on his good side for years. He'd shown me respect, if not friendly camaraderie, and I hoped it would work in my favor.

◉

Being a man who wasn't needed on the floor, Thompson didn't have to arrive so early. Nevertheless, he was routinely one of the first people—if not *the* first person—to arrive every morning. The plant's business day began at eight o'clock in the morning, and at one minute past the top of the hour, I was dialing Thompson's direct line, knowing he'd be there awaiting my call.

My heart raced and the palms of my hands were slick with sweat. I couldn't understand this attack of nerves when I was calling simply to rectify an error, to receive what I was owed.

The phone rang only once.

"John Thompson."

That was his way of answering the phone. Never a "Hello," never a "Good morning." Just his name, said in a sharp, surly way to confirm that you'd reached the man you were looking for, and that he had little time to waste.

"Hi, John, it's Dan."

"Dan! I was expecting a call from you. Great to hear from you. How are you feeling?"

"I'm feeling great, John," I replied with my stock answer to the million-dollar question on everybody's tongue. "Feeling better every day."

"Good, good. All's well here, but we miss having you around!"

"Yeah, I have to say, it's strange not getting up and going to work each day. I hope you're all getting along fine without me."

"Well, the guy who took your spot caught on slowly, though he's improving every day," Thompson replied with a chuckle. " He's got a big pair of shoes to fill. I mean, for a while, I wasn't sure if we'd survive without you around."

"Oh, I'll bet," I said.

He was laying on the flattery, as I'd expected he would. Then he made a light groaning sound, as if he were stretching out, getting comfortable in his chair, and continued. "Yeah, it was definitely strange without you coming in every day. And not having you around to train the new guy made it *pretty* tough. You know?"

"Sure, I suppose."

"No one knows the job like you, and we had to figure out how to train him on the job while making sure production stayed on target for the first quarter. We definitely could have used you!"

Oh, is that so? So sorry, John! Didn't mean to make things so difficult for you while I was enjoying an upside-down cold plunge on Christmas Eve and napping away nearly half a year in a hospital bed!

"Me too, John, me too," I calmly replied, tempering my boiling blood as best I could. I twisted the phone cord between the fingers of my right hand, rubbing it against the softening calluses. "Things sure didn't go the way I planned. I mean, nobody wants to end up in a hospital bed for that long."

"Of course not. It's not good for any of us. Hell, we were paying for a good chunk of those bills!" He laughed, like it was just a joke.

What is the point, John? Why are you rubbing this in my face? What are you setting me up for?

"Ha, ha," I said, not bothering to make the fake laugh even the least bit convincing. "It cost me quite a bit too. Money *and* months of my life. I mean, it's hard to imagine that me almost dying would work out well for any of us."

"Well, I'm just glad you're okay, Dan. It's really good to know you're okay now."

There was a brief pause in the conversation. He knew damn well why I was calling, but it was going to be up to me to broach the subject.

"Um—speaking of money, John, there is one thing I do need to discuss with you. I've been getting my pension checks in the mail now for the last couple months, and my daughter has been depositing them for me. But now that I'm receiving them myself, I've noticed that the amount is off quite a bit from what I'm due. See, my biweekly check should be for $342, but I'm only receiving about $274."

"*Ahh* . . . well, Sally did let me know about this, and, well—I hate to say it, Dan, but because you didn't complete the full work year prior to your retirement, you never actually qualified for the full amount due to you had you actually worked *through* the final year. You probably know this, but the percentage of the full pension amount you receive decreases substantially in early retirement, and it decreases with every year subtracted from the full thirty years necessary to *obtain* your full pension."

There it is: the bombshell. They've gotten me on a technicality. They found a way to pick a drowning man's pockets.

"*Son of a bitch!*" I shouted. "You mean to tell me, John, that you're *penalizing* me for getting into an accident that nearly *killed me?*"

"Dan, take it easy," he said in a forceful, authoritative manner. There it was! The tone he'd spared me for so many years, now utilized. "*How* or *why* you didn't finish out the year doesn't matter. Whether you clock out early to sit on a beach in Maui or end up in your unfortunate situation is not our concern. We can't start making exceptions for you or for anyone. What kind of precedent would that set? What kind of message would that send?"

"Oh, I don't know—maybe that you give a shit about the people who helped keep that company going for *three goddamned decades!*"

"You don't think we care? We covered you while you were out cold, we spent a fortune training your replacement, and we got hit with a massive increase in insurance rates this year because of the expenses you racked up. Not even the doctors thought you'd pull through, yet we chipped in and helped out—"

"Well, what the hell were you going to do otherwise? Sneak into my room and pull the plug on me?"

"Dan, listen—Dan, I really feel for you. I do. I care a lot about you, and I hate the position you're in. But we can't pay you based on a full thirty years."

"Great," I snapped. "Glad to clear that up. Another thing, though. I did some number-crunching and this whole thing seems pretty strange. I was getting $571 per pay period when I was working, which means my full pension would have paid out $342. So even if I retired a year early, I should still be getting ninety-four percent of—"

"*Ninety* percent," Thompson interjected. "Retiring early by a year drops you down to ninety percent. Hasn't been ninety-four percent in I don't know how many years."

"Jesus, John. All right, fine. *Ninety* percent, then. That would still put me at—"

He cut in again. "Dan, Dan, hold on. I'll explain to you the situation." Sighing, he began, "I did some digging a while back and found that for the first three years you were employed by Murphy Industries, you were actually part-time. That means that for three years—"

"Wait a second!" I shouted. "I worked my ass off during those years on the floor, and I had a lot of months where I was putting in full-time hours *despite* working another full-time job!"

"I understand, Dan, but you weren't paying into a pension plan then. In fact, you didn't begin contributing to your pension until February of 1966. I do apologize for the confusion and lack of communication on our part, but considering that you stopped working in December of 1992, minus the three years of hourly work, you only qualify to receive eighty percent of your full pension."

Stunned and speechless, I breathed heavily into the receiver, trying to come up with the proper words. Meanwhile, Thompson shifted gears and affected an overly polite demeanor as he attempted to humor and placate the man whose life he had just derailed.

"I'm truly sorry about all this, Dan. You must understand that this isn't easy for me to say to you. And I'd love to help you any way I can. Now, you know we've filled your position, but this summer we will have numerous openings in production, as well as a position available in shipping and receiving. Any available position, it's as good as yours."

"At reduced pay, I suppose."

"Well, we certainly can't afford to pay management salary to non-manage—"

I'd heard enough. There was no way I was returning even at a higher rate of pay. "You know what, John? Fuck your offer. And fuck you. I'll see you in court."

I slammed the phone receiver with such force it cracked the cradle.

6.

"I'll see you in court." An idle threat from a powerless man. Thompson must have had a good chuckle at that one. A meeting of less than thirty minutes with legal counsel informed me that I didn't have a chance in hell of winning, and considering Murphy's deep pockets to combat me in court, it would be a waste of time and money to attempt a lawsuit.

Besides, I'd already lost enough money on the Florida house. After eight months of making payments, in addition to the sizable down payment, I had no choice but to walk away from the mortgage.

I had just enough income to live on—and that was all I could say I had going for me. Otherwise, I was broken and defeated; I had fallen lower than I'd been prior to the accident, as I was too poor and too disillusioned to feel any hope for *the future* I'd been dreaming of since I was a young man.

So I sat around the house for much of the summer. I'd never realized just how hot it could get some days. Despite that, most of the time, I stayed indoors and stared out at my ex-wife's house and felt sorry for myself.

◉

Several months later, on an unseasonably muggy, sticky early morning in late September, I followed a path up the forested slope behind my house shortly after sunrise. I'd walked it countless times. Often, I'd stomp through the stands of white pine and scraggly black spruce and pretend that I was not on a hill in Granbury, Vermont, but scaling a peak in Glacier National Park or ascending a mountain in the Cascades of northern Washington. The fantasy was most believable on cool, misty days—the kind when thin swaths of fog drift from the forest floor to the height of the treetops, the way I'd imagine it must be in the Pacific Northwest. I'd imagine that the well-worn trail would lead me out of the woods and past the tree line to open slopes of alpine grass strewn with lichen-covered boulders. On my way to the summit, I'd scramble above the low rainclouds and find blue sky on top of a pale sea of cotton balls pierced by snow-capped peaks. The sun would shine down and I'd cast a shadow on the clouds below.

Instead, the height of the land simply leveled out near a band of small white granite cliffs less than a dozen feet tall. There was no view at any time of the year. Still, I hiked up behind my property at least once or twice a week. It was pleasant—much cooler among the evergreens, and the earth, black and spongy and fertile, squished underfoot like foam rubber. Sunlight rarely penetrated the thick forest, and the shaded soil overflowed with scuttling black ants. The entire hillside, in fact, may have been one enormous anthill. Often, I would see holes and scars in the ground where black bears had pawed away to unearth and snack on the insects, and that day, the forest floor was littered with such signs.

But though I saw the marks, trudging along with my head hanging and eyes cast to the ground, I was too far gone into my own mind to notice or care. Winter was coming, and despite the surprise heat wave sweeping through Vermont, it would be bitterly cold soon. Instead of passing the months lounging in tropical comfort, I'd be stuck indoors again, stoking the woodstove, emerging only to shovel the walk and clear the driveway every now and then.

With no job to return to and no real wintertime hobbies, it figured to be the longest, loneliest season of my life.

I really couldn't think of many reasons to go on living. *Well, the kids*, I supposed. My granddaughter too. But even the thought of my own flesh and blood was barely consolation—hardly reason enough to temper the morbid, sad thoughts racing through my mind. The kids almost never visited and rarely invited me over. It made me unhappy, but I understood. I had been in their shoes once too—a young, working family man who never had enough time to give his folks a ring. No time for the important stuff, and barely enough time for all the other bullshit.

I scrabbled up to the top of a small protruding knoll and then descended a few feet into a small depression in the hillside.

Just then, I caught sight of a young black bear sitting splay-legged, like a giant, hairy toddler, beside a rotten stump. He was small and lean—a yearling, well under a hundred pounds, I estimated—and had probably only been separated from his mother for a couple months. But his dark coat appeared full and glossy, and he clawed at and swatted the earth with the energy of a puppy.

The young bear had dug up the mossy ground between his hind legs, and much of the soft stump had been reduced to a pile of mushy sawdust. Millions of carpenter ants burst forth from the excavation like lava from a volcano. Frenzied, they scattered and climbed over one another as the bear greedily spooned them with his long claws and slurped them down as if he were a glutton inhaling handfuls of popcorn in a dark movie theater.

Only about twenty-five or thirty feet separated us, but somehow he remained unaware of me. A slight headwind blew in my direction, carrying my scent away from the bear. But the fact that he hadn't seen or heard me proved just how immersed he was in his feast—and that meant he'd be really startled if he discovered me.

For a minute, maybe two, I lingered motionless and unnoticed, all the while regretting that I'd left my scarcely used Canon Sure Shot at home. Then, wishing to leave the bear in peace, I attempted to back away, taking shallow breaths and slowly pressing my heels into the ground to ensure that I kept my footing. But I stumbled backward over a fallen log and fell hard on my back, failing to catch myself as I collapsed.

"*Oof!*"

Being defenseless and vulnerable for even a split second sent a wave of panic through me as I scrambled back to my feet. But as scared as I was, the wide-eyed black bear was even more terrified. He nearly tumbled backward himself as he rocked on his haunches and rolled over onto all four legs. Then he tore away up the hillside, making as much racket as an entire herd of white-tailed deer crashing through the brush. In seconds, he was out of sight, and silence returned to the woods. The hurricane of ants swirling over the ground would live another day to rebuild their subterranean city.

Poor guy, I thought. *He'd struck the mother lode of ant-hills. He knows as well as I do that winter is right around the corner. And I had to go and interrupt his meal while he's trying desperately to fatten himself up for a long winter's nap.*

At that moment, like a bolt of lightning, an idea struck me. An absurd, *insane* idea that practically made me laugh out loud for having even thought of it.

Wiping sweat from my brow, I stood by a bunch of withering ferns and caught my breath for a few minutes. My heart still raced from the commotion. I squinted into the distance, trying to see if I could spot the black bear. I could not. For a moment, I watched the survivors of the bear attack on the anthill, already scurrying to rebuild their devastated society. Then I retreated to the house.

After changing out of my sweat-soaked shirt, I toasted a few frozen waffles for breakfast. My mind raced as I ate, cramming huge forkfuls into my mouth, barely tasting the butter and maple syrup. By the time I polished off the last bite, I'd made up my mind. It was worth a try. At least worth discussing.

Who knows? Maybe it could work.

I called a friend, Dr. William Butcher, to invite him over for dinner that evening. He gladly accepted. Then I poured the last of the morning's coffee into a travel mug and drove downtown to Martin's Food Market and the hardware store.

7.

Dr. Butcher and I had been friendly for many years. We met shortly after my wedding, when he opened the doors to his medical practice in Granbury and became my family physician. He had a few years on me but still continued to practice, though infrequently and on a loose schedule, making occasional house calls to established patients.

As my dedicated longtime doctor, he had been one of the only people to visit me regularly in the hospital during my coma—and the only person to visit who was not related to me. Due to several bouts with anemia, I required a pair of red blood cell transfusions. Butcher, blood type O negative and the picture of health, donated both times.

"Almost every time I went to the hospital to see you, Dr. Butcher was there keeping watch, asking the hospital staff questions about your progress," Mary told me after I returned home. "He really cares about you, Dad."

He *did* care—so much, in fact, that he became something of a nuisance. After I awoke from my coma, Butcher sat in on most of my rehabilitative sessions, chiming in with his opinion on nearly everything the therapists and neurologists had to say. They bristled at his irritating presence but tolerated him, thinking that I wished him to be there as my physician and caretaker. This was not true. But, not wanting to offend or hurt him, I passively accepted his involvement and figured it would all be over soon.

However, after I returned home, Dr. Butcher continued to stop by daily to check up on me. At last it became too much to bear. After a week of turning him away from my dooryard, I gently explained to the doctor that if I needed him, I'd be sure to call.

Now, months later, I needed him.

When I invited him over, he initially suspected something was wrong with me, but I emphasized that I merely wished for a social visit. A lifelong bachelor, Butcher was known to be reclusive, generally shut in at his cavernous home when not with patients. But he was by no means antisocial—quite the contrary, in fact—and was happy to accept the invite.

We'd be having a feast, the first decent meal I'd cooked for myself in a long while: crackers with ham and cheese, salad with dandelion greens and late-season vegetables from my daughter's garden, roasted potatoes, baked trout fillets, asparagus, and, if we had room, an apple pie I'd picked up in town.

More punctual than most doctors, Butcher showed up at seven o'clock on the dot, just as I finished setting out the spread on the seldom-used dining table.

"Expecting a crowd tonight?" he asked with an amused grin as he surveyed the meal, removing his tweed cap and adjusting his wire-rimmed glasses.

"Nope, just the two of us," I replied as I grabbed a pair of beers from the fridge, passing one off.

"Celebrating any particular occasion?"

"Maybe." I grabbed some crackers and invited him to sit down.

◉

Quite some time had passed since we'd enjoyed a real visit. William hadn't stopped by since I'd sent him away months earlier. Now we had a chance to chat and catch up.

I told him about my pension issues and the shabby, unjust treatment I'd received from my longtime employers as he sat quietly shaking his head between bites of dinner. And despite the fact that he surely was in a better financial position than me, his problems sounded similar to mine—namely, listlessness brought about by not having enough tasks in a day to fill the hours. Another common drawback of old age. Going on house calls gave him some sense of purpose and interaction, but it did not suffice.

"For the most part," he said, hands resting on his full belly, "I tend to wonder what use I serve anymore. To myself and to others."

"Why don't you get out of here?" I asked. "Leave town for a while. Travel."

"I've traveled plenty in my life. Problem is, it's true what they say. You can't run away from yourself. Your problems always find you." He paused, staring into the bottom of his drink, lost for a moment in his own past. "And besides," he added, "this is my home, and this is where I belong."

"Well, you won't find a place where you're more well liked," I offered as consolation. "You've been a fine doctor for a lot of years. And you still are. There isn't a person in this town that would have anything but kind and appreciative words for you."

"That's nice of you to say," is all he said in reply, a hint of a smile on his face. "And by the way, that was a *fine* meal."

"Glad you liked it."

I retrieved a couple more beers from the fridge. He gladly accepted his.

"So, William, I have something else I'd like to mention to you while you're here. I figured that you might be able to give me some advice, considering your medical expertise."

"Of course. I'm happy to help."

I adjusted myself in my seat, cracked my beer, and took a deep swig. Then I leaned forward and looked him square in the eyes.

"Something I didn't mention earlier is that last year, before my accident, I put a down payment on a new home, down in southern Florida. I was planning to spend my retirement there, since I've got no use for freezing cold New England winters. I made about eight months' worth of payments on the place too. But, as you can probably guess, that's not happening now. I couldn't afford it on my reduced pension, and I had to swallow the loss of the money I already sunk into the place.

"Needless to say, I'm not in any position to relocate at this point. I'm stuck here, whether I like it or not." I let out a long sigh. "Even if I squirrel away as much money as I can, I figure it will take me at least ten years, maybe more, to be back at the point I was before the accident."

"I'm awfully sorry to hear about that, Daniel." Dr. Butcher's forehead was scrunched, and his eyes were knitted in concern and pity as he sat back and let me speak.

"As you well know, I nearly drowned last winter. It was horrible, of course. But it was the *cold water* that kept me alive for more than a half-hour—even when I couldn't breathe! It sounds like science fiction, but it really happened. I mean, the human body—it's miraculous what it can endure!"

"Indeed," he agreed, nodding. He knew I was leading up to something, and he wanted me to get to the point. So I took a deep breath and spilled it.

"So here's what I got to thinking today. If I could survive a horrible wreck and total oxygen deprivation while dangling upside-down in a river, then why couldn't I survive, I don't know, some form of suspended animation, or rather, *hibernation*? Like a bear? Bears are mammals; we're mammals. Shouldn't we be able to tolerate a long sleep if our body temperature is reduced in a controlled, safe, supervised environment? I know it sounds like sci-fi nonsense—but I *experienced* it firsthand. What do you think?"

My eagerness starkly contrasted with Dr. Butcher's calm, thoughtful demeanor. Decades of work in medicine had given him the ability to mask his thoughts and always front a neutral appearance. But the surprise I'd given him was evident in his eyes. No, this was not what he'd expected to come out of my mouth when he'd agreed to have dinner, and I suddenly felt embarrassed as I waited for him to stand up, call me nuts, and walk out of my home for good.

Instead, he took a sip of beer and glanced off to the side. It seemed as though he were about to laugh, but then he smacked his lips and said, "Induced human hibernation, eh? Sounds pretty . . . *crazy.*"

I laughed. "I'll admit, it's crazy, all right."

"Pretty unlikely too. We may be mammals, but we've developed and evolved very differently from bears. Our bodies aren't meant to endure such long periods of inactivity. And even bears aren't true hibernators, despite what most people think. No, bears are deep sleepers—but they are not hibernators."

"Regardless, Will, I don't think we need to use the bears' model of winter sleep as a prototype for our own. For example, a bear's body temperature does drop slightly, but not dramatically. Plus, they sleep in a warm, comfortable den. I guess what I'm talking about is something closer to a cryogenic freeze than an actual mammalian hibernation. You know? Look at me—I was frozen alive without oxygen for a half-hour. Who's to say that, with mild anesthesia and careful supervision, I couldn't stretch that out over the length of a winter?"

"Daniel, are you really saying you would *want* to be frozen alive for an entire winter?" he asked incredulously.

"If it were painless, sure," I answered. "Absolutely. After I passed out in the river, I don't remember a thing. Months passed like *seconds*. I lost consciousness, and the next thing I know, it's springtime and I'm looking at the ceiling of the hospital. It was nothing more than a long, restful, dreamless nap. It was like returning from the dead."

William shook his head and leaned forward in his seat. "But *why* would that appeal to you?"

His direct question deserved an honest response. But suddenly, I found myself tongue-tied and feeling ashamed. Clearing my throat, I began to feel tears welling up in my eyes and a lump rising from my chest. Was I about to cry? I hadn't shed tears in years, and probably hadn't cried in front of anyone else since I was a child.

But I pulled myself together and took a deep breath. "I'm not happy. In fact, to be perfectly honest, I'm as miserable as I've ever been in my life, and sometimes—a lot of the time—I get to thinking that I'd be better off dead. And—it's not that I'm even *afraid* of dying, but I am afraid of hurting the people who love me. So I stick around. Maybe . . . maybe I don't have much to look forward to. That I can deal with. But I'm dreading winter. I can't take the thought of being trapped here when I was so close to getting out. This hibernation is the only escape I can afford."

I'd been staring at my hands in my lap, and when I finished speaking, I glanced up at William, only to look away immediately toward the living room behind him. My embarrassment was total and only grew worse when he pushed himself out of his seat, walked around the dining table to me, and placed a kind hand on my shoulder. He must have read the shame on my face.

"We call this 'passive suicidal ideation' . . . it's so much more common than you think, and nothing to be ashamed of. But you should get some help, Dan, beyond what I can offer. I'd be more than happy to recommend some excellent doctors who specialize in the kinds of—"

"No, no," I cut in, standing up beside him. "I don't want help, and I don't *need* help. I'm beyond help at this point. Considering the way my life has gone in the past year, sitting down with a doctor and talking about my problems isn't going to solve any of them. All I want is a damn break."

"A break isn't going to solve these issues," he argued. "As I was saying, you can't run from your problems—and you sure as hell can't *sleep* through them."

I shook my head. "Look—I have something to show you. Follow me."

I walked past the doctor and led the way through the kitchen and down into the mudroom, grabbing a flashlight on my way through. Then we went out the back door into the yard. In the dusk, a large, rotund male woodcock was shuffling and dancing his way through the grass, and we damn near stumbled over him before he flew straight upward with a thunderous beating of wings, landing in the top of an apple tree.

After nearly having simultaneous heart attacks, Dr. Butcher and I had a good laugh and continued on to the outbuilding. While I used it as a woodshed and storage area, as well as a place to tinker, it was, in actuality, a fairly large sugar shack I'd built twenty-five years earlier.

Regrettably, no sugaring equipment was ever installed, and it was never used for its intended purpose. Each spring, while sugarmakers across the Green Mountains bustled in the woods collecting sap, the time to take on a new hobby never presented itself to me. Plus, I realized too late that I simply didn't have sufficient sugar maples on my property to support a large-scale operation. And without any access or right-of-way to a plentiful sugar bush, I gave up on the idea altogether, dismissing it as a foolish, passing fancy.

Still, the sugar shack was a great building with plenty of space, and was well adapted to other purposes.

A single halogen work light, attached high up the wall to an exposed two-by-four, illuminated my creation from that afternoon. It sat in the center of the floor: a crude pine box that looked very much like a wide coffin without a lid. It had a big interior with ample room for a human to lie in, a slanted backrest, and an elevated platform to support the neck and head. Waterproof plastic sheeting lined the interior so as to prevent the leakage of the ice water in which the user would be submerged.

"This is just a prototype. Plus, I plan to build a larger second box to nest this smaller box inside of," I informed William as I explained how my contraption worked. "The gap between the larger box and the perimeter of the smaller box will be lined with a thin layer of insulation, and it'll be filled with crushed ice and rock salt to help keep the water inside the smaller box chilled—kind of like a hand-crank ice cream maker. But," I added, "the insulation should also help prevent the ice-water bath from freezing solid during colder nights. At least, that's the idea."

If Dr. Butcher had found it difficult to maintain a poker face when I'd first revealed my plans, it was now downright impossible. His mouth opened in complete astonishment as he slowly circled and examined the hibernation casket sitting on the dusty dirt floor of the sugarhouse. Then he knelt down and touched it gingerly, as though he were examining the sarcophagus of an ancient Egyptian king.

"You're serious about all this," he said, looking at me in the pale glow of the work lamp. "You're absolutely dead serious about this." He stood up again and shook his head, deep in thought, and then walked past me out onto the lawn. I followed.

"I don't know about this, Dan. I just don't know."

"Put some thought into it," I entreated as I followed him around the house. "For me."

"Oh, I will. I will absolutely look into this. Thank you for dinner, Daniel. It was wonderful."

"Thanks for coming, and thank you for hearing me out." We shook hands and he entered his Oldsmobile. Before he pulled away, though, he rolled down his window and called out to me.

"Daniel? One thing before I go. In case there is a chance we can proceed with this demented experiment, you will want to begin increasing your intake of calories and fat immediately."

8.

Several days later, on a midweek afternoon, William called me at my home. It was quite a surprise, since I'd not expected to hear from him so quickly, if at all. But he sounded upbeat—enthusiastic, even.

"Daniel, how are you?"

"Fine, fine. Yourself?"

"Couldn't be better," he answered before diving right into the purpose of his call. "Listen, I've got some interesting things to report. First, I'll just come out and say this: I think we can do it."

"No kidding?" I replied, sounding as eager as a child. "You really think so, eh?"

"I don't see why not. I have my doubts, of course, but I do believe it can be done."

The doctor wasn't humoring me. Apparently, he had obsessed over the idea since our meeting, poring over every book he could find on the subjects of torpor and hibernation at the library and in his own personal collection of biological and medical tomes.

"I believe we can lower your metabolism to a mere fraction of that of a normal human," he explained, "as my aim will be to lower your heart rate to only six to ten beats per minute. Once you are unconscious and your body temperature has begun to drop using cold-water immersion and cooled intravenous saline, I will continually administer an adenosine receptor agonist, a drug targeting the A_1 adenosine receptor—a G-protein-coupled receptor that—"

"Hold on, a drug?" I interrupted. "I thought that once I was sedated, drugs wouldn't be necessary. Which drug?"

"A drug, yes—multiple drugs, actually, but in light doses. First, the A_1 adenosine receptor agonist, DPCPX— otherwise known as . . . let me check my notes . . . *dipropylcyclopentylxanthine*—will need to be administered every three days. At least, that is my assumption. I will administer it more frequently if I find it to be necessary. Or less frequently, if possible."

"But why?" I asked. "What exactly will this do?"

"Essentially, by utilizing the drug to agonize the A_1 receptor, we will be inducing a state of torpor in your system by sending a signal to your hypothalamus. Obviously, torpor and hibernation are not natural states for the human body, but by utilizing continuous doses of DPCPX, we should be able to trick your body into 'naturally' lowering its core temperature."

"The ice water, though," I continued to question, "would that not be enough to lower my temperature?"

"Yes, of course, it certainly will lower your body temperature. But *without* the A_1 agonizer, your body will enter hypothermia, as the human body does when faced with a severely lowered core temperature. And in such a state, you can only survive for so long. *With* the DPCPX, your body will—rather, *should*—accept the temperature change without putting up a fight, so to speak. Furthermore, the agonizer will help to regulate your breathing and stimulate brain activity during torpor.

"Now, regarding the ice bath," he continued. "Without it, your body may not be able to achieve such a low core temperature, nor maintain it. The external cooling, as well as the intravenous cooling saline, will allow us to coax your body's temperatures down. Additionally, the cold submersion will further slow blood flow and reduce your metabolism, allowing you to survive the long winter on stored calories."

"I understand, Will," I said, telling only a half-truth. "A moment ago, though, you mentioned 'multiple drugs in light doses'—what is the other drug?"

"Phenobarbital," he answered. "I am not one hundred percent certain that the cold submersion and the A_1 adenosine receptor agonist will be sufficient to keep you in a state of hibernation, so I will be administering minute amounts of the barbiturate intravenously. My hope is that it will be needed no more than once per week; if I find that you do not need the drug, I will reduce the dosage and increase the time between administrations. I may find that, in time, it is not needed at all. But I'd feel best if we at least start by using it."

"Mmm," I grunted, disliking what I'd heard but having no basis for argument.

The doctor continued, "If you are able to evacuate your bowels prior to undergoing the procedure, we should have no problem with peritonitis, nor abdominal sepsis. But I am concerned about the possibility of urosepsis, so we'll have to take proper precautions."

"And that would be?" I asked.

"We'll need to utilize a catheter, at least for the first week or so."

It was as though he could see me cringing through the phone.

"But don't worry! By the time it is put in place, you will be fast asleep due to the initial anesthesia. You'll never even be aware of it."

"That's a relief," I said, still squirming in my seat.

"I figured you'd feel that way. Now, once we get you put under, I'm going to need to closely monitor your condition, especially during the first hours and days. I will be by your side around the clock early on. I am confident that you will emerge from the forced hibernation feeling spry, alert, and rested—a bit weak, but you should recover more quickly from this than you did from your coma, as the reduction in your metabolism will limit the amount of oxidative stress on your body, as well as the small amounts of sarcopenic muscle loss you'd otherwise naturally endure. Plus, it is my theory that, on ice, your muscles will atrophy less than they would at normal body temperature."

"Okay, that's good news. Now, how exactly will you be monitoring me?"

"Ah, good question," William said. "Blood pressure, oxygen saturation of the blood, pulse, brain activity, and core temperature will all need to be watched constantly, as any abnormal signs could be indicative of imminent . . . tragedy. In short, you will be very close to death when we put you in this catatonic 'deep freeze,' so to speak. You have to understand that you will be, to my knowledge, the first ever human to intentionally lower his or her body temperature so drastically. And when treading uncharted territory, you are always flirting with death."

The risk of death was something I was ready to deal with. Besides, I was as unafraid of dying as any man could be. Hearing the words come from the mouth of a trusted doctor, however, sent a chill down my spine just the same.

I sighed and tried to reply, but could think of nothing to say. Sensing my waning enthusiasm, Dr. Butcher attempted to perk me up. "I have to stress, Daniel, that you will be in the best care with me. I will be by your side throughout. In addition to monitoring your vitals, I will ensure that the temperature of the ice bath remains between thirty-five and forty-two degrees, ideally, and is adjusted as needed to prevent frostbite. And it goes without saying that I will resuscitate you should your safety come into question at any time."

"You certainly seem to be keen on this whole thing, William."

"Of course!" He laughed. "I haven't felt this enthusiastic since medical school, and to think that I could be a pioneer in a medical procedure that is so *daring* . . . it's really a gift that you're giving to me. I appreciate it immensely, and I promise that I will not let you down."

William Butcher had been my doctor for decades. He'd treated me, Sandy, and my children. In fact, my son Ralphie perhaps owed his life to Dr. Butcher, who'd treated him in infancy during a midnight fever approaching one hundred six degrees. Coincidentally, his technique during the late-night house call had been to place little Ralphie into a bathtub of cool water to drop his fever. I knew I was in good hands, and I didn't need his assurance—but still, the boost of confidence sealed my decision once and for all.

"So now it's time to develop an eating plan for you to follow for the next couple months. And also, you'll have to inform any family and friends who might worry about you or wonder about your plans."

My heart sank in my chest. Now *that* was something I hadn't thought of. I thanked the doctor, said goodbye, and hung up.

It was a beautiful afternoon. The broad leaves of the tall, centuries-old maples along Old Stage Road were just beginning to change color, and the afternoon sun brightened the rusty leaves. It was funny how the signs of autumn, though they signaled the coming of winter, were always a welcome sight.

If things don't go as planned, this might be the last fall I live to see, I thought. *So I might as well take a walk and enjoy it while I try to think of how I'm going to break the crushing news of my bizarre plans to my children.*

9.

What could I say to Mary and Ralphie? Could I find any way to rationalize something that seemed so irrational? With the accident and the subsequent coma, I'd already put them through a full season of worry, and now I was primed to do it again—and on purpose, which somehow made it worse.

If I could let them know just how miserable I felt, then perhaps they'd understand. But I wasn't particularly interested in revealing to the kids how truly pathetic a person I was.

At the time, I believed my life to be tragic. It was not a dramatic tragedy, though. It was not a plane-crash-in-the-ocean-type tragedy, where everyone would mourn my sudden loss; it was not a sudden-rare-disease-type tragedy, where everyone would pity my unenviable and inexplicable condition. It was the quietest type of tragedy: a silent, invisible tragedy of loneliness and unspoken pain, where no one visits bearing flowers and sharing tears. A tragedy where no one asks how you are getting along, because they don't suspect a thing is wrong. And when nothing is wrong, people simply do not care.

Ultimately, I decided that I wouldn't share my troubles or my plans with Mary and Ralphie—and especially not with Sandy. Shortly before the big freeze, I would call the kids and say that I'd be taking a months-long road trip through Canada. I'd be vague on the details, and I'd have William stow my pickup to evade suspicion. I'd let them know the truth come springtime.

And if I didn't survive, I'd leave for them a letter explaining the whole crazy scheme and exonerating Dr. Butcher of any guilt. Butcher's lawyer would secure it for me.

It was a simple, foolproof plan. I was happy to have some simplicity in my life.

My new diet was a different matter altogether, complicated and costly. As if the low pension payments weren't bad enough, the amount of food I was required to devour was practically draining my monthly income. Carbohydrates had become my new best friend; lean meats, dairy protein, and giant egg omelets complemented my pasta and bread intake. At the very least I'd *tripled* my intake of food, as I aimed to ingest six to eight thousand calories each day.

And it worked—my weight shot up from one hundred sixty-eight pounds to nearly two hundred ten in just over two months' time. Quite a lot of weight for a small-framed guy under five-ten in height.

⊙

Just over a week before the start of my "Canadian adventure," I visited Mary's house for a holiday feast. Elsie, my five-year-old granddaughter, rushed to greet me at the door. "Grandpa!" she shouted, jumping into my arms.

"Hello, dear," I said. "Are Mom and Dad in the kitchen?"

"Yes," she said, "making a big dinner."

"Oh, really? What's the occasion? Is there something going on tonight?" I asked in mock confusion, tickling her belly so she'd know I was playing.

"Grandpa," she said, laughing, "it's Thanksgiving! You know that."

I took off my jacket and boots and carried Elsie into the kitchen, where Mary and Nate were at work finishing dinner. I hadn't seen them since early October, and as Mary turned to greet me, wiping her hands on her apron, she exclaimed, "Dad!" and then stood back to appraise me. "What happened to you?"

"Hey, Dan," said Nate, greeting me before I had a chance to reply. He smiled and shook my hand and then glanced at my recently developed potbelly. "You look like you've been eating well."

"Yes, well, I've been developing a love of cooking," I said, rubbing my protruding belly with both hands. "And a love of eating as well."

"You've been overdoing it," Mary cut in. "I've never seen you so heavy. How could you do that to yourself?"

"Honey, don't you worry about me. I'm eating well and packing it on for my road trip. I don't know if I'll be eating quite as well or how long it will be between meals when I'm out there traveling."

"Dad, you're going to be driving through plenty of towns. Last I checked, Canadians still have supermarkets and restaurants, yes? Where will you be going where you won't have access to food?"

A couple hundred feet from my kitchen.

"I'll tell you all about it over dinner."

And I did. As I crammed myself full of plate after plate of stuffing and potatoes and turkey, I spun a wonderful tale about a voyage I could only dream of.

"I'll be leaving next week—Monday morning, crack of dawn," I began, making a mental note to stash my truck at Will's place on Saturday so that it would look like I left early—just in case Mary decided to drop in unannounced. "First, I'm going to travel the eastern part of the country by heading up along the Saint Lawrence River."

"Are you going to stop over in Quebec City?" asked Nate. "The old fortified part of town is beautiful, and the waterfall outside of the city is really something to see in wintertime."

"Yes, I suppose I might, if I can afford to."

"Well, it shouldn't be too hard to get a cheap place to stay," he said between mouthfuls of food. "With the strong US dollar, you can probably get a motel for as little as—"

"No, no," I interrupted. "I mean, I might not be able to afford the *time*."

Now it was Mary's turn to jump in. "What do you mean, Dad? You've got all the time in the world."

"Yes, Mary, it's true that I will have a lot of time, but even still, I need to keep moving if I'm to cover the distance I have planned." I was getting a bit impatient, as I wished to explain my fake itinerary uninterrupted. "Can I please continue?"

"Sorry, Dan," said Nate. "Go ahead."

"Okay, as I was saying, I will be heading northeast, along the Saint Lawrence. Within about, oh, two or three days at the most, I should be around the entrance to the route that heads north up toward Labrador City. You know," I said, looking at Mary, "I've always wanted to travel up that way, but your mom thought it would be too difficult to take young children with us! Anyway, I should make it up to Labrador by day four. There are some motels I can stay at, and if not, I'll just put the pop-up tent in the back of my pickup and wrap myself in thermal blankets real tight."

"Sounds like something you'd enjoy," said Mary before turning to Elsie and saying in the next breath, "Els, eat all your peas, please, or you don't get any dessert."

"Yes, it will be," I said. *It really would be*, I thought. "I'll check out Labrador City and then head east until I reach Newfoundland. Then I'll drive through and take a ferry to New Brunswick."

My knowledge of the Eastern and Atlantic provinces, gained by my lifelong preoccupation of studying regional maps, was coming in handy. My story sounded legit, and I was selling it quite well.

But Mary knew her geography better. Not surprising, being that social studies was in her repertoire as an elementary and junior high schoolteacher. "That's strange. Wouldn't the ferries run to Nova Scotia? It's so much closer."

"Oh—yes," I lied, "that's true. I mixed them up. Nova Scotia is where I'll go."

"And you're positive ferries run in winter?"

"Of course they do. The whole loop should take a few weeks, depending on how much I dilly-dally—"

"The national park in Newfoundland looks fantastic," said Nate. "I've seen photos."

"Yes, so have I, and that's why I'm going!" And I had once, in a book, or in a *National Geographic*. Gros Morne, it is called.

"After that, I'll head west through Quebec and into Ontario, and then I'll meander my way northwest. At some point I'll go through Banff and visit Waterton. I've always wanted to see those big mountains. Then I'll go out to Vancouver. The island, that is. Then maybe I'll head north up toward the tail of Alaska. Maybe, come springtime, I'll reach the Yukon, or maybe I'll just hop on a fishing boat and find a new career. I'll be back in a few months—or maybe I won't come back at all." I was smiling, seeing everything I'd just described in my mind, enthusiastic for a trip I wasn't taking.

"Can I come?" Elsie chimed in.

"Oh no, Elsie, this is a trip I'm taking alone," I said. "You have to stay here with your mom and dad. You don't want to miss any preschool, right?"

"But you said you won't come back." I hadn't realized she'd been paying attention. If I had, I would've chosen my words more carefully. "I don't want you to leave."

"I'm just talking, dear. Don't worry, I'll be back by April."

Even that I couldn't promise.

10.

The more I thought about it, the more my fictitious trip through Canada seemed to be my best option, even if I couldn't afford it. But I'd sealed my decision. All my bills were being rerouted to Mary, who was now a co-signer on my checking account. Dr. Butcher would be "caring for my house," I told my daughter, which was true, in a way. And he had already invested a great amount of time into his research and preparation for the hibernation—plus, he'd spent a fortune on the necessary tools and instruments.

His high-tech medical apparatus included a Holter EKG monitor, a pulse oximeter, an EEG device, and numerous adhesive thermoelectric body temperature monitors. Not to mention the opioid anesthetics, IV bags and poles, needles, syringes, a rolling hospital bed, and the dreaded urinary catheter.

The low-tech tools? Extension cords, power strips and multi-outlet converters, extra work lamps, propane tanks and a pair of forced-air propane heaters, pots and soup ladles, and thick, heavy-duty wool blankets to drape over the windows so that nobody would see the glow of the lights at night. He even special-ordered a portable tubular bathwater heater, which became quite hot within a matter of seconds after plug-in. The doctor picked up all the expenses and insisted that I not pay him back.

As for what I'd dubbed my prototype "hibernation casket" . . . William thought it would serve us well. "Simple but adequate," is how he described it. "It will work just fine."

Other than the location and the homemade box, all I had to provide was myself: the guinea pig on ice.

◉

I barely slept at all during the week leading up to the big procedure. My mind raced every time I closed my eyes. More so than in the days leading up to the births of my children or the nights following my wife's departure, my brain was a jittery, scattered mess. I was scared, excited, and conflicted about my decision. Every item in my house and each location in my town suddenly became holy, and I regarded it all with tender affection, reminiscing over everything.

There is the Italian restaurant where Sandy and I went on our first date. It's a shoe store now. And there is the office building where Mom used to work. Looks like it's almost entirely vacant!

This coffee table in the living room—I remember when Ralphie fell and hit his head on it. This old tire iron—I remember when my dad gave it to me. I should have given it to one of the kids.

There is the knothole in the ceiling that looks like a funny face. Elsie's portrait of me hanging on the refrigerator, it is wonderful. What a talented little girl! And that lamp on the bookshelf! It's a wonderful lamp. I can't recall where I got that lamp, but I love that lamp.

And so on. It was like that for everything. *Everything* had become beautiful, though it brought about only bittersweet feelings of guilt when I acknowledged that it took such extreme circumstances for me to see things as such.

I'd once read that most people who survived suicide attempts claimed that they suddenly had a change of heart and wanted to live immediately upon leaping from a bridge or a building. I knew exactly what they meant.

But, I'd remind myself, I was not going to die. I was going to *rest* and fast-forward through time. It would be like skipping part of an old movie you'd seen a million times and never enjoyed to begin with. There was a chance I'd not make it, but that chance has always existed. I could go out today and get run over by a truck; there's no point in pretending that you might not die just because you play it safe.

You will die, old man, whether or not you take it safe. Take a risk and do something crazy. Follow through on a big idea for once in your damned life.

⊙

After much waiting, Monday, December 6, 1993, arrived. Dr. Butcher had taken my pickup that weekend and parked it in his garage at home. I'd locked up and shuttered the house and sat in the dark for two days and nights to make it appear as though I'd already left for Quebec.

I was sitting in the dark on the couch, wrapped in a blanket, heart hammering away, when I heard a car roll into the icy gravel driveway. Then there was a knock at the door. It was the doctor, who'd arrived right on time, eight o'clock in the morning.

When I opened the door to let him into the chilly, dimly lit house, I was shocked to see not just one face, but two. A second elderly man, about the same age and just as bookish in appearance as William, stood behind him and off to the side, looking around nervously as if he were afraid that we were being watched.

"Good morning, Dan!" said the doctor brightly.

"Morning," I said, rushing them into the house and locking the deadbolt. "Who—who is *this*?"

"This," said William, brushing snowflakes off the front of his long woolen jacket, "is Dr. Eric Zargari, an old friend of mine I've known since medical school. Dr. Zargari is a retired surgeon and anesthesiologist from Burlington, and he's provided me with invaluable insight during my research for the procedure. I will require his professional assistance today, as well as his help in moving you from the bed to the casket. You don't think I can lift you all on my own, now do you?"

He wore a playful grin and threw a friendly wink my way, but it did little to relieve me of the feeling of betrayal.

My voice shook with anger. "Will, you should have *told me* that you were going to share this information with others. I can't have you going behind my back and telling everyone about this! What if word gets to my family? Or to *anyone*, for that matter?"

Dr. Zargari, who'd looked nervous upon arrival, now looked positively fearful as he slowly stepped away from me, avoiding eye contact as he rubbed his black-rimmed glasses on his coat. He was incredibly tall, skinny, and weak-looking—a stark contrast to the more rugged Butcher.

"Oh, no!" said Will. "I wouldn't dream of betraying your trust, and I have told no one! No one, that is, but the doctor here. He is the only person I've told, and you have my word that just as you can trust me, you can trust Dr. Zargari. He is as trustworthy as any person you could ever meet. He is a *professional* and is here on professional business, like me."

"I still think you should have told me," I replied. "I don't know this man from Adam."

"I am very sorry. I agree that I should have told you. However, I was afraid you'd argue and force me to go about this alone. While I'm flattered that you think I can do this by myself, it is not an ideal way to undertake such a foreign and risky new procedure. I've brought in Dr. Zargari for your safety and wellbeing."

Zargari, sensing that the right moment had arrived, stepped forward briskly, hand extended, and shook mine, saying, "It is a pleasure to meet you, Mr. Fassett. And let me say, I am honored to be a part of what is sure to be a historic medical breakthrough."

I returned his fey grip with a strong one, still furious but growing less so by the second. It was true that I'd perhaps overestimated Butcher's capacity to complete the procedure on his own, and it was also true that I'd neglected to consider how my limp, unconscious body would be moved from the hospital bed to the ice bath. My will to live had grown exponentially with every day leading up to this moment, and if he could help ensure my safety—well, then, what did I have to lose?

Of course, I would forgive William.

"It is nice to meet you, Dr. Zargari," I said. "If you are a colleague and friend of Dr. Butcher here, then you are a friend of mine." He smiled, relieved.

Dr. Butcher nodded, pleased, and reached into his medical bag. "Well, shall we get started? Daniel, here is your gown. Please put this on and wear nothing beneath it. Also, remember to fully evacuate your bowels."

"I already have," I said, "and I've been fasting since yesterday morning, as you requested."

"Great! Then go ahead and get changed, and meet us out back in the sugarhouse in about fifteen minutes."

◉

"Goodbye, bathroom," I said aloud as I stood on a fuzzy, brown bath mat, dressed only in an open-backed, powder-blue hospital gown. I felt like I should say something to commemorate the moment, but that was all that I could come up with. I looked at myself in the mirror. *Who is that sickly, chubby old man looking back at me from the glass?* I wondered.

I didn't care much for him, so I left the bathroom and walked through the kitchen, ignoring the few dishes I'd neglected to wash. They'd still be there in April. I slipped into a pair of rubber boots that I'd left by the back door and then, quick as a fox, sprinted to the outbuilding, following the twin tracks the doctors had left in the fresh, powdery snow. The nippy winter air felt especially frigid on my bare legs and naked pelvis.

It was never too late to have a new experience. I'd never once stepped outdoors in wintertime without pants or underwear, and now my ass was exposed to the world on a cold December morning.

Chilled to the bone, I burst into the sugar shack, quaking with cold. It felt much nicer in there. Drs. Butcher and Zargari had fired up the propane heaters, and the mercury was rising steadily. Work lamps strewn about the circumference of the room high up on the walls suffused the bizarre scene in eerie white light.

Since the building had a dirt floor, plywood sheets had been set down to make a flatter, more level surface. Butcher and I had taken care of that detail days earlier. The rolling hospital bed was set up, ready to receive me, and beside it, instruments, needles, and various tubes, hoses, and wires were scattered on a portable stainless-steel medical table. There was also a small canister of gas connected by a tube to an anesthesia facemask. The IV drip was ready to be administered.

And in the center of the room, like a sarcophagus in the middle of an elaborate, oversized mausoleum, sat the casket. The inner compartment where I would rest was half full of water, and the spout end of a lengthy garden hose attached to the spigot on the side of my house lay on the ground, ready for when the time came to add more water to the bath. Ice and snow filled the outer compartment of the casket, and beside it sat a forty-gallon plastic garbage can brimming with store-bought ice cubes originally intended for party cocktails.

How absurd to think that I originally constructed this building to make maple syrup.

The doctors, bundled in emergency-room attire and with faces concealed by surgical masks, hardly acknowledged my presence as they busied themselves preparing anesthetics and tending various monitors. Everything was just about ready.

"What's the deal with the canister and the face mask?" I asked, pointing a shaking arm. "Laughing gas or something?"

"Yes, that's correct!" Dr. Zargari piped up. "We're going to administer nitrous oxide for sedation prior to supplying pentobarbital, which is the general anesthetic that will be delivered intravenously."

"Ah." He seemed to know what he was talking about.

"Well, the time has come, Mr. Fassett," said William, addressing me oddly formally. "Hop on up here and we'll get started."

I'd hardly realized how cold I was until I slowly pulled myself up onto the vinyl mattress. I leaned back and stared up at the steam vent in the sugarhouse roof. *I should've bought an evaporator at some point*, I lamented. *I should have found a sugar bush to tap. Making syrup with the kids would have been fun.*

A long, shaky, broken sigh escaped my lungs. It was then that I realized I was shivering hard, from both cold and fright.

"Are y-you both sure that you know wha-what you're doing?" I pleaded. "Maybe we should t-talk this over—"

But before I could change my mind, Dr. Butcher slid the cushioned gas mask onto my face and pressed it down, creating a tight seal over my mouth and nose. Dr. Zargari twisted a knob to release the flow of nitrous. Then he picked up a hypodermic needle.

"Absolutely, Daniel. You are in the very best hands. Between the two of us, we have nearly a century of experience in medicine."

The skin of my left forearm was swabbed with a wet ball of cotton; then I felt a gentle pinch as a needle pierced my flesh.

"Okay, let's count backward together from ten. Ten, nine, eight . . ."

I never said a word. The world began to spin before he reached seven. Suddenly, my head felt as heavy as a sack of bricks, and a wonderful sensation, like butterflies tickling my ribs with the tips of their wings, built up within my chest cavity. I had to laugh! My mouth opened wide and I heard a hilarious, high-pitched giggle, like the whinny of a sick pony.

Is that coming from me?

"Now we're having a good time!" I heard a voice say, far off in the distance.

I felt joyful, glorious! But I was slipping away, unable to maintain my tenuous grip on consciousness—tumbling backward, carried by lead weights in my skull and cement shoes on my feet, sinking into warm, fetal oblivion.

And then there was nothing. Another small taste of death. No pain, no loneliness, no fear.

A big, empty nothing.

PART
II

11.

*H*ot. Hot. Very, very hot. Can't breathe. Gasping. So uncomfortable.

Want to move. Can't.

Want to open my eyes. Can't. Blinding redness. All I see is bright red.

Drops of liquid on my eyelids. Feels cool. Eyes burn. Finally open. Brightest light I've ever seen. It hurts to look. Nothing but whiteness. Everything is blurry. Am I underwater?

No. Breathing. Not underwater.

Focus on the ceiling. Ceiling looks strange. Wait. Where am I? This isn't my bedroom.

Okay. That's a vent. Steam vent. I'm in the sugar shack. What am I doing in the sugar shack?

It's William. I see William, my doctor. Standing beside me. His face is close to mine. What is he doing here? Am I sick? What is it he's saying? Who is he talking to?

Try to speak. Can't. Try to move. Can't!

What is wrong with me? Am I paralyzed? Am I dying?

"Take it easy, Daniel. Everything is just fine. You are doing great."

Why is he smiling?

"And welcome back."

What does he mean? "Welcome back?" *From what? Where have I been?*

How does he—

Wait. I think—

Oh. Oh. I am remembering.

Holy shit! The hibernation! I actually did it! I survived!

◉

Slowly, I came to. One eye at a time focused on my surroundings. First the right eye, then the left. I was in the casket; someone had propped me up so that I sat upright. Using a maple sap dipper, someone behind me ladled warm water over my pallid, thawing body. Pins and needles pricked my flesh, the nerves waking up after months without stimulation.

Then a splitting headache arrived. A rush of pain drove through my skull as though the fist of a heavyweight boxer wearing concrete gloves had crushed my forehead.

"*Yarrrgh!*" I groaned. It sounded awful! Jesus, a few months of deep sleep and I'd become as wretched as Frankenstein's Monster, raised from the dead, stiff and confused, without language. A fire roared in my throat, and mucus gurgled like boiling paint.

All of it was too much! The overwhelming brightness and pain, the sheer fact that I was *thinking* and *feeling* again. The wheels of my mind turned slowly, coated in wintertime rust, while my nerves reeled out of control, absorbing every stimulus and sensory detail without any ability to dampen the intensity.

I began to weep, but I was so dehydrated that no tears fell. I merely whimpered and gasped. Dr. Butcher knelt down beside me, his latex-gloved hand clutching a syringe.

"In my opinion, the endorphin production in his brain is likely lagging as a result of the freeze. So while his body is demanding endorphins to moderate the extreme pain, the supply is simply not there yet. I'm going to give your father a small dose of morphine to provide some mild relief."

He jabbed me with the stick and depressed the plunger. Instantly, warm comfort spread through my body, from the tips of my toes to my scalp.

Wait. Did he say "your father"?

Just as I'd begun to regain alertness, I fell back into a sedated dream.

◉

When I again came to, I found myself no longer naked and shuddering in the casket. Instead, I was dry, dressed in a gown, covered by a blanket, and reposed at an incline in the hospital bed. A needle delivering an intravenous rehydration solution was attached to my arm, held in place in the crook of my elbow by a single strip of medical tape. Two propane heaters on the plywood floor blasted me with warm air.

This time I felt . . . *good*. Somewhat, anyway. Very weak, but alert and rested, the way one might feel after a good night of deep, uninterrupted sleep.

Three people stood by my side: Dr. Butcher and my children, Mary and Ralphie.

If looks could kill, William would have dropped dead on the spot. Moving my head as slowly as the minute hand of a clock, I turned toward him and glared. I cleared my throat and asked in a weak, thin voice, "Where is . . . the other doctor?"

I couldn't believe those were my first words in four months. Nor could I believe the first words I would hear.

"Sadly, Dr. Zargari passed away last month."

To me, my introduction to Dr. Eric Zargari seemed to have taken place only moments before. He'd been standing right there, next to the very same bed I lay in now. I blinked my eyes and he was dead and gone—in the ground. If you'd told me on the day I was frozen that one of the three of us wouldn't be alive come springtime, I'd never have guessed that it would be Zargari.

"How?" I asked.

"A heart attack. Poor man had atherosclerosis and never had an inkling. Near total blockage in the right coronary artery. I performed the autopsy myself." He took a deep breath and cracked his knuckles. "As a doctor, I know it's important to separate my personal life from my professional life. Even still, that procedure was the most difficult I've done in nearly fifty years of practicing.

"When he passed, I was put in a difficult spot. I needed assistance, and fast—I knew we'd be reviving you in only a matter of weeks, and I had to find someone to help. With my most trusted colleague gone, I figured the safest bet would be to involve your family. So I looked up your daughter's number in the phone book and arranged a meeting. I explained the situation to her as best I could—"

"And then I called up Ralph," Mary finished. Her chin quivered. "Oh, Dad!" she cried, bursting into tears. "Have things really gotten this bad for you?"

She flung her arms around my shoulders, and I winced, still achy and sore to the touch. Her breath and tears on my neck were the warmest sensations I'd felt yet. A strong scent of flowery shampoo filled my head, dizzying me. Somehow my senses seemed to have become exponentially stronger, which was an unintended, though highly interesting, side effect.

I tried to hug her back, but I could barely lift my arms. Behind her, over her shoulder, Ralphie stood with his hands in his hip pockets, not sure how to act. Poor kid. He'd only just moved out to Montana a year and a half ago, and I'd kept him from maintaining consistent employment—*twice*. First he stayed in Vermont for nearly two months following my accident, and now he'd returned to take in this bizarre spectacle and help out however he could. He'd always been a sensitive and somewhat awkward boy, and now, nearly thirty-one years old, he'd grown into a decent man. I missed him. I hoped he wasn't becoming fed up with his tragedy of a father.

Eventually, Mary released me from her grasp. William, who ignored the sentimental display and moved about hurriedly, ran a whole series of tests to ensure that I was healthy and responsive.

"Just as healthy as a horse," he announced proudly.

12.

M y legs didn't work at all that first day, but because of
the blanket of heavy, fresh spring snow melting in
the yard, the wheelchair purchased by Dr. Butcher was left
inside my house. So with one arm draped around Ralphie's
shoulders and the other wrapped around William's, I was
slowly walked across the wet, white lawn. The first robin
of spring perched on the big apple tree in the yard, and the
sky was a brilliant blue, without a trace of clouds. While I
shivered uncomfortably in the cool breeze, I relished the
fertile, earthy smell of Vermont as it thawed.

"What day is it?" I asked as the two men carried me to
the back entrance of the house.

"April third, Dad," said Ralphie.

"1994," added the doctor. "Happy New Year! You've
been asleep for almost one hundred nineteen days.
Unprecedented!"

Mary, leading the way, opened the door to the mudroom off the kitchen. It felt as though I'd not been away at

all; for the most part, the house looked the same, though a bit cleaner than I'd left it. The dishes in the sink had been washed and put away, and the jackets and thermal underwear I'd lazily thrown across the couch were out of sight.

Carefully, I was lowered into a small manual wheelchair. It had no handles in the back, meaning it would be up to me from the get-go to move myself around. Fortunately, unlike my legs, my arms were coming around rapidly, and I was confident that it wouldn't be too difficult to get around the lower level of the house.

After some time spent quietly chatting with my children, Dr. Butcher announced, "I have to be going now, Dan. I need to work on my notes while all of this is fresh in my mind. On the dining table I've left for you a packet of nutrition guidelines and physical therapy exercises you should begin doing immediately. I'll be back tomorrow morning to check in and will continue to stop by regularly—but feel free to call me anytime!"

"Thank you, Will," I said. "I'll be sure to contact you if I have to, and I look forward to seeing you tomorrow. Around eight o'clock?"

"That's perfect. Have a good evening," he said, doffing his hat. "Keep an eye on him and make sure he follows my instructions!" he said to Mary and Ralphie.

◉

Mary was too shaken to stick around. I'd never seen her so fatigued and stress-ridden. After her emotional breakdown in the sugar shack, she had little left to give, so without a kiss, a hug, or even eye contact, she said good-bye and departed for home. Her exhaustion was matched by my guilt.

Thankfully, for my sake, Ralphie stuck around for a while. Having recently broken up with his girlfriend of six months, and having no job—the ski area where he'd worked over the winter had just closed—there was little reason for him to rush back to Bozeman.

Now alone, we sat at the dining table in awkward silence. Finally, Ralphie offered me a drink of cool water. After he filled a tumbler and placed it in front of me, he sat down again across the table. The situation was so incredibly awkward that we both began to laugh.

"Why'd you do it, Dad?" he asked, both of us grinning like idiots. "Why did you *freeze* yourself?"

I stopped laughing and stared at him blankly, not knowing how to answer. I certainly didn't have the ability, nor the energy, to articulate my self-perceived station in life. But it came out anyway, in single-word snippets.

"Desperation. Money. Sadness . . . loneliness."

He nodded his head thoughtfully. "That makes sense. I figured as much." Then he added, "I have the same problems myself. I'm pretty sure I'm not going to nap in the chest freezer in the basement, though."

I laughed at his joke, but I was earnestly surprised and taken aback by his statement. Now I was ready to speak.

"Really? Hmm. I didn't know you felt like that. I don't see what you have to feel bad for. You're young yet."

"You don't? Well, let's see: I'm in my thirties. I'm alone—*again*. I don't have a job or any career plans. And what have I ever accomplished? What do I have to show for myself?"

"You don't need to have *anything* to 'show for yourself,' Ralphie. Life isn't a damned contest. You're finding your way and doing what makes you happy. And if you're not happy, make some changes, and just take it day by day."

Yes, I was aware of my own hypocrisy. Anyone could have justifiably delivered the very same pithy, trite lecture to me, and I knew that. But maintaining a positive perspective on your own life is much more difficult than trying to force that perspective upon someone else, so I continued.

"I know you don't need to hear this, but I'm proud of you. I am proud of you, and I know your mom is too."

"What for?" demanded Ralphie, twisting the chin hairs of his rust-colored beard between a forefinger and a thumb. It was a nervous habit he always fell into when upset or in deep thought. I can't recall his tic prior to his growing of facial hair. "Really, what exactly are you so proud of?"

"You're a good man, Ralphie. It's enough to me that you're caring and decent."

He laughed through his nose. "So are *lots* of people."

"And yet there is still a shortage in the world," I countered. "Don't underestimate yourself. Things will work out for you—just be patient."

I know he wanted to say something—to argue, perhaps—but he let me have the last word. He just nodded his head affirmatively, and then stood and paced over to the counter with his back to me.

He paused for a moment and then reached for something on the far side of the Mr. Coffee, near the tins of sugar and flour. He studied the item in his hand and then turned toward me.

"When did you get glasses, Dad?" he asked, holding aloft a pair of black-rimmed bifocals.

I'd only met him once, but Dr. Zargari's face was one I'd never forget. And I immediately recognized the thick, clunky frames as his.

"Those belonged to Dr. Zargari," I said softly, suddenly feeling a twinge of sorrow at his unfortunate passing. Though I'd shared little time with him, he'd struck me as a kind, gentle man. "I guess he fixed a few pots of coffee in my kitchen. Can't say I blame him—he and William had some long nights keeping my crazy ass alive."

For a moment, Ralphie twirled the frames in his fingers thoughtfully, and then he plunked them down on the countertop.

"Well, I'm going to go visit Mom for a few minutes, just to let her know I'm around. Then I'll come back and we can see about dinner. See you in a bit." He patted my shoulder as if he were petting a newborn puppy and then walked out the door. I was alone. It felt very familiar.

Later, Ralphie ordered out and brought home a Chinese banquet. My mouth watered at the smell as he removed it from the bag.

"Oh, I'll go fix your dinner real quick, Dad," he said. "Then we can eat."

I had a can of pea soup and a mashed banana. Doctor's orders. I'd have to work my way up to lo mein.

13.

My body recuperated more quickly than I ever could have imagined. And having Ralphie around was an immense help, as he kept me motivated. Within two days, I was walking around the house with a cane; at the end of the first week, I was walking up and down the road, albeit with my son at my side, just in case I needed someone to grasp onto if my legs gave out.

By the end of the month, I was jogging. My appetite had fully returned, and my weight, which had diminished only slightly during the freeze, was returning to a safe, normal level. I began eating healthy foods again. I slept better at night. I felt alive and awake during the day, never groggy. The world looked beautiful, smelled delicious, and sounded musical—the birds in the trees, the snow melting into the rushing brook, and even the occasional jet that flew overhead. Simply put, I began to feel better than I had in twenty, maybe thirty years.

Ralphie spent a full month at home, splitting time between my house and his mother's across the street. And he covered for me with a beautiful lie, without my having to request it.

"I told Mom you slipped and fell on a sheet of ice while snowshoeing around the Laurentian Mountains, and that you spent all winter traveling with a hairline fracture in your hip," he told me. "So don't forget that story!"

Mary apparently hadn't told Sandy the truth either. In fact, it seemed Mary wasn't talking much to anyone, as she was never home whenever Ralphie or I called. The phone either rang until the answering machine picked up, or Nate would answer and say she wasn't able to come to the phone.

He sounded friendly enough, and if he knew what had actually transpired, he didn't let on. Perhaps Mary hadn't even told him the truth. I figured that she'd made up a story as to why she was angry with me to protect my secret. Nate was a trustworthy guy, and I liked him a lot—but even still, I preferred that he not know about the hibernation ordeal. The more people who knew, the more likely it was that someone would let the cat out of the bag. Even if she was mad at me, Mary was respectful enough—or perhaps just embarrassed enough—to keep her lips sealed.

Unfortunately, someone else did not.

◉

In early May, days after Ralphie's departure, I heard a knock at the door. I was dressed in a pair of shorts and a tank-top and soaked in sweat, having just returned from an hour-long jog through town.

Without hesitating or asking the caller to identify himself, I swung open the door to find a young, mop-headed man with a notepad tucked in his breast pocket and a tape recorder in his right hand, extended. Behind him, wearing a backward baseball cap and a flannel shirt, was another young man with an expensive-looking camera in his hands, a finger on the shutter button, ready to shoot.

"Excuse me, Daniel Fassett?" he asked.

"Yes." It was an instinctual response; I hadn't had any time to consider who they were or what they were doing in my dooryard.

"Oh, great. We're from *The Burlington Argus*. I was wondering, Mr. Fassett, if you might have a chance to speak with us for just a few minutes."

I was perplexed. For a moment, I thought that someone was playing a practical joke on me. "I'm not sure I understand. Why would you want to talk to me?" I asked.

"Well, we've heard that you spent the winter in—well, it sounds crazy, but in a state of *hibernation*, of sorts. And I was wondering if perhaps you would care to comment on that, or at least provide some clarifica—"

My mouth dropped open in shock and I felt my hair stand on end in terror as I slammed the door in their faces. It was not the wisest action to take—doing so was practically an admission to the charge, and if I'd just had the sense to play it cool, I could have denied it convincingly.

But no, not me.

As the door swung shut, the photographer quickly raised his camera's viewfinder up to his eye and snapped a photo of me. Instantly, the reporter started banging on the door and shouting, "Mr. Fassett, we promise that we only need a minute of your time! What was your reason for doing this, Mr. Fassett? Is it true you *froze* yourself?"

I speedily backed away from the door, then paused and tiptoed back toward it. The banging stopped for a moment; then it started again. "Is there a better time we could come speak to you, sir? Would you be comfortable if I called you from my office?"

"I have nothing to say," I yelled back. "Now get off my property before I call the police!"

Moments later I heard a car engine turn over. Peeking through a slit in the curtains I saw the photographer snapping pictures of my house and of the property as the vehicle slowly pulled away.

This was bad. I needed some time to soothe my rage and collect my thoughts.

Dr. Eric Zargari was dead, and Mary and Ralphie wouldn't tell a soul. That left one suspect. The following morning, I'd call William Butcher.

Dr. Butcher, the rotten snake.

◉

A long, restless night passed. Still, I must have slept some. I know that because when I sat down in my breakfast nook and slurped at my first cup of coffee, I saw the sugar shack door swinging wide open.

I set down my mug, sloshing hot coffee all over the table and floor, and sprinted barefoot across the dew-soaked grass to the outbuilding. Someone had pried the door open using a crowbar, and I'd slept through it. A forced entry—and yet, nothing inside was missing. In fact, everything the building contained was exactly as I'd left it. That meant that someone had broken in to take . . . what?

Then it hit me.

Photographs. They took photographs.

14.

It was not yet seven o'clock, but I knew Dr. Butcher would be awake. As I dialed his number, I took a deep breath to calm myself, but I wasn't quite sure I'd be able to hold my composure. Time and time again he'd betrayed my confidence, and in each instance, he'd come up with a good excuse. This time, however, there was nothing he could say that could justify his loose lips.

His phone rang. It rang, and it rang some more. Eventually, it occurred to me that even if he were away or asleep, his answering machine should have picked up. But it didn't. The phone rang for two full minutes before I hung up.

Maybe I dialed the wrong number, I thought. So I dialed again, paying extra attention to where I placed my fingers in the rotary.

Same result. No answer.

To pass the time, I fixed myself another pot of coffee and ate breakfast. Afterward, I called again. No answer.

I skimmed the paper and watched a bit of *The Price Is Right*. I put in another call and, as expected, there was no answer.

So I hopped in my truck and drove into town. William Butcher lived in a massive white colonial house on a small hillside just outside of the village center. Everyone was familiar with his pillared home, as it was visible from town at night due to a pair of spotlights in the front yard that lit up the façade. It was a ridiculous—not to mention, ostentatious—thing to do, but most people in town just viewed it as eccentricity rather than arrogance.

Before I even reached the driveway, I noticed that Butcher's silver Oldsmobile was missing, and as I pulled up to the house, I realized that every window was dark. Still, I went up to the front door and rang the bell several times, hoping that he'd answer.

He did not. I retreated to my home, puzzled and even more irritated than before. Three more times that evening I would phone his house to no avail. That night, I lay in bed, anxious for daybreak so I could once again attempt to contact Dr. Butcher.

But in the morning, before I could dial his number, he called me first.

◉

My phone rarely rang, especially not at such an early hour. But at half past six, the ring shattered the silence in the breakfast nook, frightening me so badly I practically jumped out of my seat.

"Hello?"

"Dan." It was the doctor. His urgent tone informed me that he was not calling with pleasant news. "It's Will. Have you seen today's paper?"

"No," I asked. "Which paper? Why?"

"*The Argus,*" he answered. "Don't you have it delivered to you?"

Indeed, I did. So without a word, I let the receiver drop from my hand; it landed with a loud clatter on the tabletop as I raced to the front door. I threw it open and there, on the stoop, was that morning's edition.

There it was, front page. Tucked away at the bottom, but nevertheless on the front page. The headline read, "A Strange Tale: Human Hibernation in Vermont's Mad River Valley."

GRANBURY — Tucked away in a gore just out of sight of the hustle and bustle of the Sugarbush ski resort, the small town of Granbury, Vermont, has emerged from another long winter.

Like many Vermonters, the residents of this small village pride themselves on resilience and self-sufficiency to survive the harsh season. For most, this means stacking cords of firewood and stocking the freezer with meat obtained during the autumn hunting season.

But for one resident, passing the winter encased in ice proved to be more desirable than sitting by a hot woodstove.

The 62-year-old man, who is not named, was rumored to have been placed into a deep, months-long state of hibernation brought about by lowering his body temperature . . . .

I stopped reading. I hadn't been named. That provided me with at least a measure of relief. But in an instant, I was full of rage and raced back to the phone. Dr. Butcher was still on the other end of the line.

"What the hell is wrong with you?" I exploded. "How could you do this to me? How could you let this out? How—"

"I didn't say a word!" he said, defending himself.

Of course you didn't.

"Then who did?" I asked, pressing him for the truth.

He sighed. "I was hoping nothing would come of this, but . . . shortly before he passed, Dr. Zargari confided in me that he'd mentioned our . . . *procedure* . . . to another colleague. A doctor, supposedly a longtime associate he'd worked with at the hospital in Burlington for many years."

"You're kidding me," I said. "The man you said was *trustworthy* and confided in *without my consent* revealed my private information."

"I am very, very sorry, Daniel. I'm completely ashamed, and am just as shocked as you are."

Another apology from someone else who'd fucked me over. It was getting old.

"I'm sure you are sorry, William, but that doesn't help me any. Who did he tell?"

"Unfortunately, I don't know," he said, and then paused. "When Eric mentioned it to me in the sugarhouse, I reacted in very much the same way *you've* reacted to *me*. I was enraged, because he'd not only gone behind my back, but he'd gone behind *your* back as well, which was even worse. Doctor-patient confidentiality is something I place the utmost importance in, and to see it violated—even with regard to such an unusual and *groundbreaking* medical process—angered me deeply."

"That doesn't explain why you couldn't find out *who* he told," I said.

"Well, that is because after I became angry with him, I asked him to leave the premises. I had full intention of getting the details from him later, but—"

"He died?"

"That very night," Dr. Butcher replied.

"Unbelievable," I said, placing my forehead in the palm of my free hand.

"He had no right, and no reason, to open his mouth—especially without your permission," the doctor emphasized.

"Nor did you, William. This is your fault."

You can only call a man out so many times, even when he is completely in the wrong, before he defends himself. It was the doctor's turn to push back.

"Now, hold on, Daniel. That's not entirely fair. Keep in mind what I explained back in December, on the day I introduced you to Dr. Zargari: I absolutely *needed* a second set of hands to properly initiate the hibernation procedure. Without Dr. Zargari, I would not have been able to do it on my own. It would have been completely impossible. I know you believed that I could go it alone, but that is because you are not a doctor. Complicated and brand-new experiments such as the one we embarked on—and completed one hundred percent successfully, I might remind you—require multiple minds working together, combining knowledge and ensuring that the patient is safe and free from harm. To that end, we were very successful in providing you with everything you needed to survive. This was your idea, Dan—but it was *my burden* to execute it successfully."

He was a smooth talker. Plus, I had to admit, he had a point. Without a second doctor on-hand, I would never have been able to pull off the winter hibernation. And though we'd been unfortunate to end up with a third party who'd opened his big, fat, *dead* mouth, it was a risk that, ultimately, had needed to be taken. Anyone could have let the secret out. It was an inherent risk that I'd not been comfortable acknowledging.

So, reluctantly, I let Dr. Butcher off the hook. "Well, I understand your point, William. And I owe you an apology for the way I snapped at you. Once again, I was quick to jump to conclusions and doubt your integrity."

"It's quite all right, Daniel," he said. "I would have reacted the same way if I were in your shoes."

"Yes, it's nerve-wracking, to say the least. I had reporters snooping around here two days ago." And then I remembered the *other* matter I had to discuss with him.

"In fact, that was when I realized that someone had let the word out about me, and I tried all day yesterday to call you. I even stopped by your house. Where were you?"

"Ah!" Dr. Butcher exclaimed. "I am sorry for that as well! Until this morning, when I saw the paper, I didn't realize that anyone aside from the doctor who Zargari spoke to knew about all this. If I had, I would've stayed home and contacted you right away, just as I did this morning. But yesterday, I was in Burlington all day."

"Oh? What for?" I asked.

"Renewing my medical license! Thanks to you, Dan, I feel invigorated and eager to practice again. It's too early for me to say, really, but I may open up my own office again. But if I do—well, it will be good to have all my ducks in a row."

"Renewing your license? I'm confused. Haven't you been doing house calls for the last several years?"

"Well," William said, lowering his voice, "it's my turn to confide something in you. For the past few years, yes, I have been visiting some of my old patients. Just a small number of them—when I have time, and at my discretion. You were among them, of course. But due to the high annual expense, I allowed my medical license to lapse when I stopped working full time and closed my office. But now—again, thanks to you—I am excited to begin practicing again in earnest."

"That's great, William. I'm happy for you. Glad that you're regaining some passion for your work. I have to admit, this whole experience has really turned my life around too. I feel so much better—healthier, happier. I feel like I appreciate life more. I just hope I'll be able to patch things up with Mary soon.

"And," I added, "I hope that there aren't any repercussions from this damned article. At least they didn't identify me, so that's something to be thankful for."

Rather than agreeing and offering me reassurance, Dr. Butcher stayed silent on the other end. Then he spoke: "Daniel . . . have you seen the whole article yet?"

"No. Why?"

"The article continues inside the paper. You should take a look."

Sure enough, at the bottom of the front page:

CONTINUED ON PAGE A7

I turned to page A7. The article continued on with at least twice as many more words than had appeared in the lead-in on the first page. There were quotes from townspeople I knew speculating on the truth of the rumor; interviews with medical professionals from Burlington and beyond, commenting on whether they thought such a procedure could be successfully accomplished. Worse yet were the two photos, one showing the interior of the sugar shack, and one showing the façade of my house.

"This is bad, William," I said. "This is really, really bad."

15.

Local gossip is a fact of small-town life. You learn young that unless you button your lip and keep to yourself, everyone will become privy to nearly all the details of your personal life. Word spreads fast, and news this sensational rarely comes along in Vermont.

Once the article hit newsstands, everyone in Granbury knew it was me. Regardless, not wanting to listen to rumors and secondhand information, acquaintances stopped by to confirm the truth. In the following days, people stopped me in the supermarket, at the hardware store, and while I was out jogging to inquire about why I did it, what it was like, and how I felt.

What could I do? The proof was there in the newspaper, front page, continued on page A7. So I owned up to it and told the truth. The word was out whether I liked it or not.

Surprisingly, I never heard from Sandy. On occasion, I'd see Mary's car parked in her driveway, but she never came over to see me. I kept trying to call her, and even stopped by a few times, but she'd cut off contact. Nathaniel dropped by from time to time with Elsie, though, which I appreciated. He remained friendly with me, though we never discussed Mary beyond my asking how she was doing and his replying, "Fine." Elsie was none the wiser to her grandpa's newfound local celebrity.

Aside from my ex-wife and my daughter, everyone treated me decently. I'd expected to be shunned and treated like a freak, but instead, many people let me know that they were relieved I was okay and that they were there for me if I needed anything. It was heartwarming. It made me feel bad because I'd believed nobody cared when, in fact, they all would've been happy to help. And after the initial hysteria died down, they gave me my privacy. They also helped to ensure that I *kept* my privacy once the state and national media came to town and curious tourists started showing up.

It didn't matter who came to town. Whether they were from WCAX in Burlington or CNN's New York City bureau, nobody could get directions to my house from the residents of Granbury. Reporters had to work diligently to find my address, and if they did show up, I locked the doors and turned out the lights. The sugar shack remained bolted shut. When tourists asked the locals, "Can you tell me how to get to that frozen guy's house?" they responded, "Who?" Handwritten signs appeared on the doors of the general store, the IGA, Martin's, and the post office declaring, "No Directions to the Hibernation House." I felt safe, like a Kansas farmer hunkered down in a storm shelter while a tornado ripped by.

Of course, it couldn't last.

◉

Never underestimate the public's voracious appetite for a juicy and bizarre story. Tabloid rags at the grocery store checkout are dedicated to pointless celebrity gossip— who was arrested for drug possession, who gained or lost weight, and so on. My story was far more interesting than that garbage, even I had to admit. And the people who took interest in my story ranged from brain-dead bottom-feeders who wanted to know if I shit ice cubes or if my testicles froze and fell off to doctors and NASA scientists who were captivated by the medical miracle. There were hoaxers, conspiracy theorists, and even a tiny cult that sprung up proclaiming I was Jesus reincarnate. I ignored them entirely. Some of them sought me out; almost all failed and gave up quickly.

But the people most eager to find me were the ones who identified with me. The ones who understood me and knew why I did what I did without needing any explanation. The ones who felt marginalized and alone. People tired of living but too afraid to die.

One day in late July, while out jogging on a buggy backwoods dirt road, I realized I was being followed. In the distance, about three hundred feet behind, a man shadowed me. Thinking it was about to be my first encounter with paparazzi, I immediately stopped and sprinted back to confront him.

But he carried no camera, no notepad, and no tape recorder.

Great. A stalker. He's going to kill me.

"Hey, you there," I said, trying to catch my breath. "What do you want?"

The scrawny, sweat-soaked young man, dressed in a long-sleeved, white cotton shirt and blue jeans, simply stared bug-eyed, stammering. Then I noticed tears welling up in his eyes.

Just as he appeared about to bawl, he swallowed and said, "Mr. Fassett, I've come a long way to see you. All the way from Toledo, Ohio."

"Are you one of those cult people?" I asked. "I'm not Jesus, you know."

"No, no," he assured me, wiping a greasy clump of hair out of his eyes. "Those people are nuts."

I nodded, agreeing.

"No, I wanted to talk to you, sir, because—well . . . I was wondering if, perhaps, you might help me out."

"I can't help you," I said in a strict, firm voice. "Really. I don't have anything I can offer you. Whatever you need, you should look elsewhere."

"But I can't!" he replied. "You're the *only* person to have ever done what you did."

"So?" I pressed.

"Well, I was thinking you could help me because . . . I'd like to be the second."

"Shit, kid!" I yelled. "You're coming to me looking for some bullshit chance at *fame?* You've got to be out of your fucking mind!"

"That's not true!" he said, and once again, he looked as though he were about to cry. He struggled for words, his face flushed and strained. Then, instead of speaking, he yanked up the left sleeve of his shirt and bared the soft underside of his forearm. Red scars of various lengths crisscrossed the flesh at random angles leading up to the crook of his elbow, where the last slash stopped short of the bulging ulnar vein. In addition to the bright-red lines, a handful of faded circular bruises, like slowly healing wasp stings, polka-dotted his flesh.

"I'm not coming to you for fame, Mr. Fassett."

"Call me Dan," I said. I didn't like being called Mr. Fassett.

"I'm coming to you for help. This is what I did to myself last winter, while you were sleeping. After I began to bleed out, I suddenly panicked. I wrapped up my arm and went to a hospital. I spent months in a psych ward. And now that I'm out, I don't want to live. I'm trapped, Dan. I need a break. You once needed to give your mind a rest. It's my turn."

He began to sob and shudder. He wasn't much older, if at all older, than my son. I put my arm around him, and we walked back to my house, where I invited him in for coffee and conversation.

◉

His name was Jeremy Clark. He sat on the old, brown couch in my living room while I took the wooden rocking chair. It was a sweltering, humid day, but we both sipped at hot cups of coffee while he spoke and I listened.

As Jeremy's story unfolded, I felt more ashamed than ever of the pity party I'd thrown for myself the past winter. To say he'd been dealt a lousy hand in life would be an understatement.

Not long ago, he'd been happily married to his high school sweetheart with a six-year-old son. They rented a nice, affordable two-bedroom apartment. He worked in retail; his wife worked as a waitress. "Nothing fancy, but it paid the bills, and we liked what we did," he explained.

Then, one night, at a four-way intersection in Perrysburg, a speeding Peterbilt blew through a stop sign, crushing his small Toyota. His wife and son, both seated on the passenger's side, were killed instantly, while Jeremy ended up in the hospital in critical care.

"If they truly wanted to be humanitarians, they would have let me die," he said. "I don't even remember the accident. I remember driving. We were almost home. Then I blinked and opened my eyes, and my life was ruined."

Following a week or two in the hospital, Jeremy was freed from his bed and his morphine drip and released. But with hairline stress fractures running throughout his ribcage and a severe neck sprain caused by whiplash, he felt overwhelmed by pain—both physical and emotional. A call to the doctor quickly resulted in a call to the pharmacy, where he was given a prescription bottle of hydrocodone.

When it ran out, the doctor authorized a refill. Jeremy learned that doubling or even tripling his doses provided more relief. But the pain continued, and it required little lobbying on his part to persuade the doctor to give him a prescription for something a bit stronger: oxycodone.

"I ate through that bottle of oxy like Pac-Man swallowing dots," Jeremy said, shaking his head. "When I contacted the doctor again, he agreed to give me one last script—but he warned me to slow down, because that was it. He was cutting me off. And the bottle only lasted me three days."

After that, Jeremy hit the streets of Toledo and Detroit to get his oxy. But prices were high, and supply was low. To save money and trouble, a "friend" turned him on to oxy's cousin, heroin.

"At first I was sniffing it, and then I was smoking it. Hell, to this day, I've never even smoked a cigarette. After that, I started slamming." Then he clarified, "Using a needle," displaying for me his lacerated and track-marked forearm. "I didn't care what happened to me. I figured eventually I would overdose or get a bad batch, but it never happened. Instead, I ran out of money. I tried to kill myself, but then I lost the nerve and rushed off to the hospital. Then *they* shuttled me off to a psych ward, where I had to sit in a circle with other patients, talk to a counselor . . . you know how it goes."

I didn't, but I said, "Sure."

"And all this," he exclaimed, "while going through withdrawal! After a few months, they let me go. I thought they'd figured I was all better, but no, it was just that my mom couldn't pay anymore."

"How long have you been out?"

"Well, about a month or two. No, maybe it's been closer to three. I don't know. Long enough to relapse. But I read about you while I was in the clinic. I said to myself, 'Now there's a guy who knows what he's doing. There's a guy who will get me.'"

In a way, I did "get him," but I certainly couldn't relate. My life had been a goddamned enchanted dream compared to his.

"So now you want me to help you out by putting you into hibernation," I said, clarifying the obvious. "You know, winter is a while away. You still would have to wait about three months, maybe a little more, before we could do this."

"It'll give me something to look forward to," he said. "It will help motivate me to keep going and stay clean."

"It's not something you *should* 'look forward' to, though, Jeremy. You have to realize, three or four months is a long time to be out, but to you, it will feel like hardly any time has passed."

"I don't care," he responded as he slugged the last sip of coffee in his mug. "I really don't. It's something I need. When I wake up and realize I've made it through however many months and that spring has arrived, and that I've stayed clean for nearly a year, hell, it won't matter to me that I spent part of the time sleeping through it. It will be time for me to start my life again. Or at least, to give it a shot."

He was determined. I had to give him credit. But I didn't understand why he didn't want to start working on that new start *right now*, so I asked.

He merely replied, "I'm not ready," and I pressed no further.

Jeremy had arrived from Toledo by Greyhound, which had dropped him off in Rutland. He'd hitchhiked east on Route 4 and north along Route 100 and then hoofed his way into town, where he'd found out where I lived from someone.

"Who?" I asked, extremely curious to know.

"I don't know," he said, shrugging his shoulders incredulously. "I didn't get his name. Some old guy downtown. I was so nervous I didn't even really look at him."

I was disappointed, but it was just as well. No sense in harboring resentment or even suspicion toward a townsperson. In addition to the many residents who respected my wishes to be left alone, there were bound to be some who simply didn't think twice when doling out personal addresses to complete strangers.

Jeremy was short on cash, so I went upstairs to my bedroom and pulled out a lockbox containing emergency cash from under the bed. I handed him six crisp twenty-dollar bills, which was enough for a night's stay at the Downtowner Motel, a few cheap meals, and a bus ticket back to Toledo. He left me with the phone number for his mother's house, where he'd be staying.

"I don't know if I can help you, Jeremy," I said as I dropped him off at the Downtowner. "But I'll see what I can do. I will be in touch, and I wish you the very best."

He shook my hand and said, "If nothing else, thanks for listening." Before he entered the motel office, he turned and waved goodbye and flashed a friendly smile. That smile, belying all the pain he must have felt every waking second of every day, broke my heart.

I hadn't spoken to Dr. Butcher in a couple weeks. It was time to reach out.

16.

"That's a very sad story. I really feel for him. But I don't know, Daniel. It seems kind of risky to do this again. We were successful once, but it might not be a good idea to push the envelope."

"I understand, William. I just thought that it would be nice to help this kid out. He really could use some help. He's in a bad way. And considering you did this once, I figured you might feel more confident the second time around. You know what they say: 'Practice makes perfect,' right?"

"Yes, well, I am quite confident in my abilities. However, I am concerned about how other people—other than you, that is—might react to the procedure. Different body types, different weights, various ethnicities, and so on. We haven't had an opportunity to test this on any-one but you—a healthy, medium-framed, white male nonsmoker."

"Older, too. Don't forget that. If I can survive this as an old man who's already had a prior brush with death, I'm fairly certain a young man could."

"A young heroin addict? There are many negative effects that heroin can have on the body that aren't always immediately apparent—"

"*Former* addict," I said, hoping he could stay clean over the coming months. "And he's smaller-framed than me and thinner than I was a year ago, but there should be plenty of time for him to bulk up. And besides, I'm worried about him. He has less to live for than I did last year. That's putting it mildly. But the fact that he's reaching out to us and asking for help means he still has some will to go on with his life. In his mind, taking an extended break from life will help him out, and I think the psychological boost could really do him some good."

"You could be right about that, Dan—it really has done a world of good for you. And to date, I haven't noted any adverse effects of it in any of my examinations."

"Absolutely. I'm walking proof that good can come from induced hibernation."

"Indeed, you are. But here's the other thing: You said earlier that he has no money, correct?"

"Correct."

"He's living with his mother, correct? The one who couldn't afford to pay for his stay in the psychiatric hospital?"

"Yes."

"Well, then, this is the other big problem. Who, exactly, is going to pay for all this? Last winter, all of the medical equipment and drugs were paid for by *me*— not to mention all the unpaid time Dr. Zargari and I put in! Now, of course, Daniel, please don't take that to mean that I feel you owe me anything. Absolutely not. I consider what I did a service to you, as a friend, and I remind you that it was my privilege to take part in the whole adventure."

"I know; you've mentioned that. I'm glad we went through it together. But don't you think that doing this a second time might allow you to work on the procedure and learn more from it? Doesn't it appeal to you from an academic standpoint?"

"I can't afford it this winter, Dan. I just can't spare the thousands of dollars and hours I put in last winter."

"The kid can't pay, William. It's out of the question; he told me so himself. And I don't have enough to part with either. I guess . . . I guess we'll have to call the whole thing off. He'll be disappointed, but maybe I can find some other way to help him out."

"Hmm. Now, wait a minute. There *is* a way we could subsidize young Jeremy's treatment without forfeiting any of our own income. It would be pretty extreme, but it could be done. I'm not sure you'd go for it though."

"What do you mean? What's your idea?"

"Well, if we had other interested parties—relatively physically fit candidates who wanted to take part in the procedure and were willing to pay—then we could cover the cost of treating Jeremy. We could effectively subsidize his stay while serving others and covering all of our expenses."

"What? You can't possibly mean that. A minute ago you were protesting that it wouldn't be a good idea to 'push the envelope,' as you said, and now you want to bring more people into the fold? Get out of here!"

"I'm serious, Dan. I do want to help this young man every bit as much as you. You're absolutely correct—his situation is dire, and we might be the only ones who can help him get his life back on track. This is the only feasible way to go about this. Unless you can think of a better idea."

"No . . . no, I suppose I can't. But what about the legal implications? And who will we find that would actually want to *pay* for this?"

"Don't worry about a thing! I have a lawyer friend down in Boston who can draft a contract for us that will free us from liability in case anything goes wrong. And as you know, I am once again a registered medical practitioner in the state of Vermont, so I can offer the winter hibernation service through my practice's limited liability company—we'll just keep it hush-hush."

"'Hush-hush'? Why? So there *are* legal issues here?"

"No, no, I just don't want the state's Board of Medical Practice down my throat. Trust me, neither do you. I'd rather keep them out of the sugarhouse altogether. Their interference could cause major problems, for us and for our patients. And as for finding patients, well . . . you can leave that to me too. I just need you to build us, oh, say, four more caskets."

17.

Asurprising number of people applied for the four open spots. When I asked William how he'd spread the word, he merely explained that, as a doctor, he had contact with many other medical professionals all around the country, who in turn knew other physicians, surgeons, psychologists, and so on. He put the word out that we were looking for referrals for several worthy candidates for hibernation—and since our story was so well known, it proved to be quite simple. Doctors and patients alike were eager to take part.

Stacks of applications came pouring in to the doctor. Each application included medical and personal information, along with a personal statement outlining the individual's reason for wanting to go through with the procedure. Dr. Butcher insisted that he, being the professional, would take full responsibility for carefully reviewing each and every one. When the list was narrowed down, he began phone interviews to finalize the selection process. Within eight or nine days of our conversation, he mailed me a copy of the application of the first person he'd chosen: Lauren Andrews, a widowed forty-four-year-old black woman from New Haven, Connecticut.

A widow. I'd had a feeling that this might be the only type of person we'd attract—someone who had lost a loved one, either by tragedy or divorce, and wanted to hide from misery in the shadows of oblivion.

A chill ran through me. Suppose someone enjoyed the respite we offered so much that they decided to make it permanent. If one of our clients committed suicide, wouldn't *we* have blood on our hands?

No, no. I remembered how I felt after I came out of my hibernation, refreshed and invigorated. Downright happy! I was happier now than I'd been in a long while.

At least, I had been. For a few months, I was happy. But now, this whole business of offering hibernation services was beginning to drag me down. I'd have five frozen bodies in my sugar shack this winter, and they'd be my responsibility—partly, anyway.

Well, it's too late to back out now.

◉

It took another week for William to decide upon a second patient, and only another three days after that to determine a third. As with the first patient selected, Butcher provided me with copies of the applications and letters. Affixed to one, I found a sticky note that read, "I hope

you're familiarizing yourself with your future tenants!"
There was a smiley face at the bottom of the note. I was
not amused.

The second candidate was a wealthy fifty-two-year-old
white man from Las Vegas named Kevin Christopher.
He was a mountain of a man, weighing more than two
hundred twenty pounds and standing almost six feet four
inches. I'd have to modify one of the caskets to accommo-
date him. Unsurprisingly, he was recently divorced.

The third person Dr. Butcher chose was a young woman—a *very* young woman of mixed race, with a Japanese
mother and a Caucasian father. Only twenty-three years
of age, Rebecka Pollard was an aspiring doctor and medical student from Orange County, California. In the past
year, judging by the personal statement she'd written, she
had developed an unhealthy obsession with my story. "I
have always been interested in cryogenics, and I've followed your story from the start with great interest. Now
I am excited to be a part of medical history!" she wrote,
underlining the word "history."

It seemed to me that the doctor was being careless
in his selections. I noticed that he'd chosen three people
of widely varying physical characteristics, which made
it obvious he was basing his choices largely upon what
would help him most with his research and not necessarily upon who needed the most help.

Disgusted, I tossed the girl's application on the messy
kitchen table and walked over to the fridge to grab a beer.
We still needed one more volunteer to pay for Jeremy's

procedure, and I couldn't imagine who would be selected for the final spot. As I cracked open the bottle, I glanced out the window to see someone trudging up Old Stage Road in the pouring rain toward the house.

18.

Unlike the previous autumn, September of 1994 had been exceptionally cool. With temperatures in the fifties during the day and hovering just above forty at night, it felt as though October had arrived a month ahead of schedule.

Still, the man slowly slogging through the mud was dressed only in shorts, a T-shirt, and a flimsy, clear plastic poncho. No umbrella—and no rubber boots, for that matter. His sneakers appeared to be soaked through.

He walked with his head down. Through the thin fog, I could make out that he was an older man with salt-and-pepper hair, a white beard, and Coke-bottle glasses. It was likely he kept his head down just to keep raindrops off his lenses so his vision wouldn't be completely obscured. He looked familiar, but I couldn't be sure of who he was.

As he approached my house, he paused in the driveway and looked up, as if to appraise whether he really wanted to see me or if he should just turn around. His decision to approach was sealed when we inadvertently made eye contact as I peered out the window.

It was then that I recognized him, a fellow local who'd made a big splash in local and regional news: Joseph Gooley.

Everyone knew his name. But unlike my claim to fame, Gooley's was much more sinister. Shortly before noon on a bright summer day in 1961, in the living room of his mother's house where he lived at the time, Gooley was caught bare-ass naked with a trio of neighborhood children: two seven-year-old boys and a nine-year-old girl. A father of one of the boys, who lived only a few houses over, had been out looking for his son, who'd skipped out that morning on his daily chores. Upon spying his kid's Huffy tucked behind the garbage cans alongside the Gooley residence, he poked his head in the front door, which Joe had neglected to lock.

The ensuing brouhaha became the stuff of local legend. The father, an ex-military townie cop named Doug Sloan, rushed Gooley and grabbed him by the scruff of his fat neck and hurled him, completely nude, through the screen door. He flopped onto the porch and skidded down the front steps, landing scraped and bloodied at the edge of the sidewalk.

But before Joseph had a chance to blink his eyes and catch his breath, Officer Sloan was on top of him, pummeling his face with his fists. The noise of Sloan's cursing and the bawling of the children—not to mention, the shrieks coming from Gooley's busted craw—caught the attention of every person within a thousand feet. And when a few other parents on the street realized exactly *why* an off-duty town cop was beating the shit out of a naked civilian in broad daylight, they jumped in on the action.

For more than five minutes, Gooley lay sprawled at the base of a flailing, furious dog pile. The bloodthirsty mob drove their fists and stomped their feet into every inch of his body until, at last, an on-duty officer slowly pulled up and half-heartedly subdued the crowd. Unconscious and mangled almost beyond recognition, Joe was cuffed, tossed into the back seat of the police car, and driven down to Rutland, where he spent two weeks in the hospital. After that, he was thrown right into jail and eventually sentenced to twenty-eight years—no parole, no commutation—to be served at the penitentiary in Springfield.

◉

He rolled back into town in 1989, a pale, thin, and disfigured shadow of the pudgy man who'd been banished all those years ago. His mother had passed away just a year prior to the end of his sentence and bequeathed him her home, as well as enough cash from stocks, bonds, and whole-life insurance to last him the rest of his life. So in addition to the fury that the townspeople still harbored toward him, Joe also got to face the animosity of those who couldn't believe such a rotten bastard had fallen over backward and landed in a pile of money.

Verbal abuse rained down on him every time he showed his face in public. The best he could hope for from others was a silent look of disgust or an indifferent snub. For five years he rarely left his house.

Sometimes I had to wonder just how much penance a person must pay before he has atoned for his crimes. I couldn't help but feel just a trace of pity for the frail old man who was tromping up my porch steps. But then, it wasn't my kids he'd raped. It wasn't me he'd threatened to kill if he couldn't have his way with me.

Maybe there was no atonement.

Joe Gooley became known to everyone in town at the age of thirty, when he'd been caught in the midst of his horrible crime, but I'd known him for much longer. He and I were the same age and went to school together starting in kindergarten. I never cared much for him. While he and I weren't the most popular or outgoing kids in town, we never bonded as outcasts, and were never friendly. Frankly, I found him to be extremely strange and also irritating.

But that didn't stop me from being decent to him. Hell, in fourth grade, I saved him from major injury—maybe from death. We were outside during recess, a whole slew of boys, playing "king of the hill," when someone decided it would be fun to play "king of the bleachers" at the nearby baseball diamond. The wooden bleachers were fairly tall, approximately ten rows standing around twelve feet high. Not the best place for a group of kids to scrap and fight—especially considering that there was no railing at the top. In lieu of an adequate barrier, there was just a two-foot-high seat back.

Ten or twelve of us rushed to the base of the bleachers. Nobody particularly liked Joe, but he came along anyway. Largely ignored by the rest of us while we fought and scrambled to reach the pinnacle, Joe easily coasted to the top row.

"I won! I won!" he yelled, waving his arms high in the air. His shirt lifted up showing his fat, pink belly. "I'm king!"

"Bullshit!" yelled another boy near the top, who reached up and swiped at his ankles. Chubby little Joe Gooley's weight shifted back, and he swung his arms in big circles, like an enormous bird trying to take flight. But he failed to regain his balance. It seemed as though he were destined to tip over and plunge head-first into the hard-packed gravel below.

Fortunately for him, I too was near the top. With a rush of adrenaline, I reached out with one hand and snagged him by the cuff of his blue jeans; as he continued to topple, I grabbed his other leg. I was amazed I could get such a strong grip so quickly, and on such a heavy guy. He dangled upside down, his rotund face turning purple as a turnip as he screamed, "*Put me down! Put me down, goddamnit!*"

I couldn't believe what he was saying. Did he not realize what had happened? Did he really not understand that plummeting more than a dozen feet and landing on his head could kill him, or at least paralyze him?

"Someone get around the other side and help me out!"
I shouted. Immediately, two boys leaped from the bleachers and scrambled around to help, ostensibly more concerned about the trouble we'd be in if we let a classmate
get injured than about the fat kid's safety.

My fingers and forearms ached from the strain of
holding Joe aloft, and just as he began to slip from my
grip, someone called out, "Okay, let him go!"

I released him, and my classmates caught him by the
shoulders before dumping him in a heap on the ground.
Flush and sobbing and sniffling back snot, Joe pulled
himself up out of the dust in the shade of the bleachers
and immediately ran back to the schoolyard, where he
ratted us out.

All of the boys, including me, were given five lashes
apiece and had to miss recess for a month. I never spoke
to him again.

Many times in the past three decades, it had occurred
to me that the world might have been better off if I'd just
let him fall. How could I have known then that I was
saving the life of a future child rapist? At that age I don't
even think I had a clear understanding of what that was.
I was aware that some older guys were pervs, sure. I'd
had a guy corner me at an isolated urinal at Fenway Park
when I was nine to watch me take a leak. It was weird. But
what Gooley did? I couldn't have imagined it in my worst
nightmares. At least, not when I was so young.

It was pointless speculation. If I'd seen him die, I would
have had to live with that for the rest of my life. Instead,

I saved a life. It was the only life I'd ever saved. Not many people can even say that much: *I saved someone's life.* Figures I'd go and save a worthless one.

Now, here he was, more than fifty years later, standing on my porch in the rain.

◉

I opened the door. He stood there, soaked and shivering. He lowered the hood of his poncho, which hadn't kept his head dry at all. His graying hair was matted and tangled, and the white beard on his face, with a gross-looking six-inch goatee dangling from his chin, dripped like a leaky faucet. The beating he'd taken all those years ago had left his nose crooked and his jaw misaligned, and his mouth hung open, displaying yellowed teeth. It looked as though an aspiring wizard had attempted to transform a mountain goat into a man with iffy results.

"What can I do for you?" I asked after a brief silence.

"H-hi, Daniel. Remember me?" is all he said.

"Sure do. What can I do for you?" I repeated.

He cleared his throat. "Well, sir—I hear things on the TV about your freezer operation you got going. And I was thinkin' that maybe, well . . . I was thinkin' I might be able to *pay* you a bit of money if you can do that for me this comin' winter."

Interesting proposition, Joseph.

"Come on in," I offered. "Kick off those muddy shoes on the doormat here and shake out that poncho before you come inside."

I didn't really want Gooley in my living room—in fact, I wasn't crazy about having him in my house at all—but I allowed him to take a seat at my nook, which was close to the front door. I didn't offer him a cup of coffee, in case he decided to get comfortable, so we cut right to the chase.

"People around here don't care much for me at all," he said. "I don't blame 'em, either. I did do a bad, bad thing a long time ago. People don't forget them things, and they don't let you forget none, either."

Nodding my head quietly, I let him continue.

"So I heard about what you got workin' on up here. Figured that for a guy like me, who don't ever leave the house anyway . . . maybe you wouldn't mind puttin' me up for the winter."

"Why, though?" I asked. "Why would you want to do that?"

He just shrugged and said, "Better than livin'. Prolly better than dyin', too."

"And why should I do this for you?"

"Because, I said, *I can pay you*," and he leaned toward me and enunciated the words to show his impatience. I was taken aback by it, but then realized I shouldn't expect stellar manners from an ex-con rapist hermit.

"Well, turns out," I replied, "that I may be able to help you. *Maybe*." I sighed, incredulous that I was considering his offer at all. "Believe it or not, I just might have a few guests up in the sugar shack this winter. But I don't know, Joe—I'd have to run it by my, uh, partner in all this. He's the one who evaluates all the potential patients, and you'll probably have to fill out a bunch of paperwork. And," I added, "you need to know that my partner is charging eight-thousand dollars for the procedure."

"I got money," he said with a faint grin. "I'll give you *fifteen* thousand."

I tried to hide my shock, but the fact that his smile widened told me that I'd done a lousy job. "Write down your phone number for me, and we'll be in touch," I said, handing him a pen and a scrap of paper.

He wrote it down next to his name. Then he put on his poncho and shoes and walked out the door without even saying goodbye.

◉

As soon as Gooley was out of sight, I hopped on the phone and dialed up Dr. Butcher.

"William," I said as soon as he answered, "It's Dan. Do you remember Joseph Gooley?"

"What?" he replied, flustered and annoyed. "The molester? Of course I remember him! Why do you ask?"

"Because I just had a little visit from him."

19.

When I mentioned that Gooley wished to be frozen, William seemed hesitant, which was understandable. The man's reputation was burned into our minds, and becoming the handlers of his frozen body for four months would force us to confront an awful mental image over and over.

Of course, when I mentioned the money, the doctor quickly changed his tune. Gooley's status immediately went from "maybe" to "shoo-in."

But I wasn't terribly happy about Butcher's attitude toward Gooley. Before I disclosed the proffered payment, the doctor merely said, "Perhaps we could take him. I wouldn't mind observing the effects of the procedure on an older man in somewhat poor health.

"Besides," he added with a curt laugh, "if the creep dies in our hands, we'd be doing the world a favor."

I didn't find that quip to be terribly funny. "Pretty sure that violates the Hippocratic Oath, Doc," I scolded.

"Of course. I say that only in jest," he replied, backtracking. "Can he pay?"

"Fifteen grand, William. I didn't ask for it. He's the one who pulled that number out. I think he really wants us to do this for him."

"In that case, we'd be crazy to say no!"

◉

It was the doctor's responsibility to contact all the patients to arrange payment and travel details, collect legal waivers, and provide proper nutrition guidelines to be followed during the months leading up to hibernation. It was my duty to prepare the sugar shack.

Unlike the previous year, the building was soundproofed with insulation, and the windows were slathered with multiple coats of black latex paint to prevent any natural light from entering—as well as to keep any artificial light from escaping. I added numerous locks to the door and cleared the entire room of all my personal belongings, ensuring adequate space for the five caskets and all the needed medical equipment. Most of my things I just piled up in the basement of my house or tossed in a heap in the yard and covered with a tarp. Firewood was stacked in neat rows close to the bulkhead, and lawnmowers were parked in secret in the old barn on Sandy's property across the street. I did it one day while I was sure she was out. I figured she'd never even notice.

Lastly, I situated additional lamps around the perimeter of the room, close to the ceiling, spaced about thirty inches apart. The interior of the sugar shack was lit up like a tiny sports stadium. Dr. Butcher, who collected the payments, reimbursed me from the bank account he'd set up solely for our winter business. Though I objected that he hadn't added me as a partner to his LLC, nor as a signer to his business bank account, he insisted that it was best for tax purposes. He was entirely transparent with all the money coming in and going out, which reassured me.

By early November, we were all set to proceed. Amazingly, despite the slew of doctors who were now privy to our plans, the media hadn't gotten wind of our latest scheme. William drew up a schedule: We would admit each patient one by one, in order of selection, two days apart. This would give us enough time to sedate and induce hibernation in each person in private, with our full attention. Plus, it would give the doctor a full day to monitor their vital signs and ensure that they were responding well to treatment. We would begin on Monday, December 5, 1994, with Jeremy Clark. We would admit our final patient on Tuesday, December 13. That would be Joseph Gooley.

20.

November flew by, the days passing by like speeding cars on a highway. If I thought I'd been nervous the previous year, it was nothing compared to how I felt as this December approached. One day, I was riffling through my file cabinet, reviewing my finances, when I chanced to find a real estate brochure from the realtor in Key Largo. I flipped it open to see a photo of the cottage that I, Daniel Fassett, had proudly owned for several months. Many months had passed since I'd allowed myself to think of that place. Suddenly, I longed for it now more than ever.

◎

On December 4, Jeremy Clark of Toledo, Ohio, arrived via train in Montpelier. William picked him up in his car and drove him to the Downtowner, where he'd reserved a room, all paid for by me and the doctor—or, at least, by our other clients. Jeremy was to fast that evening and meet Dr. Butcher at seven-thirty the next morning in the lobby. We'd begin the procedure at eight o'clock sharp.

Ten minutes before the top of the hour, there was a knock at the door. I felt like I was experiencing déjà vu from the previous year as I arose from the couch to receive my visitors. Half expecting to see the ghost of Dr. Zargari shadowing William, I was relieved to find that it was, in fact, young Mr. Clark in tow.

He looked much different than the last time I'd seen him. Not to mention much healthier and in much better spirits. The gaunt, sweat-soaked tragedy of a man riddled with track marks and razor wounds had been replaced by a bright-eyed and fleshy boy brimming with enthusiasm. I shook the doctor's hand and then the hand of Jeremy, who gripped tightly and looked around the room with an exorbitant sense of awe.

"Great to see you, Daniel!" he said. "Wow . . . your place looks exactly as I remember it!"

I chuckled, a little taken aback by his reaction, and said, "Well, it's only been a few months. To tell you the truth, I haven't really changed the place much in the past twenty, thirty years."

"It's great," he said, grinning. "I've really been looking forward to this day a lot. I can't thank you guys enough."

"In that case, there's no time like now to get started," said William. "Your gown and robe are over there," he said, motioning to the folded clothes we'd set out on the dining table. "You can change in the bathroom, and then we will walk out to the sugarhouse together."

"Great! But where do I put my stuff?"

"I set up a row of chests out in the shack to be placed by your, uh, 'bed,'" I replied, "and I set it up with a lock combination that is the same as your birthday."

"Sounds good," he said, disappearing into the bathroom. It took him barely a minute to emerge wearing the thick, brand-new fleece robe we'd provided on top of his gown. He nodded. "Let's do this."

◉

The three of us walked to the sugar shack single file; I took the lead, followed by Jeremy, with Dr. Butcher in the rear. It was cloudy and cool, and very little snow was on the ground. What snow there was had thawed and refrozen numerous times, making for a slick path across the yard. Jeremy, having no boots, wore a pair of worn tennis shoes and slipped several times.

"Oops! Ha ha!" he laughed after each minor spill.

The boy is off his rocker.

Inside, I flipped on the lights and illuminated the room. A single hospital bed and medical table sat in the center, situated in the approximate spot where my casket had been placed the previous winter. A set of shelves for extra supplies had been constructed against the far back wall. Along each of the other two walls the caskets were lined up—two on the left wall, and three on the right. At the foot of each hung a clipboard with sheets of paper for note-taking and brand-new meat thermometers to measure the temperatures of the ice baths.

"Wow," said Jeremy. "Impressive. Looks so different than it used to."

"Did I bring you back here this past summer?" I asked. "I don't remember doing that."

"Newspaper photos," he replied.

"Right." I'd forgotten about that.

The doctor slipped off his jacket and hung it on a hook by the door, squeezed his hands into a pair of latex gloves, and then began to collect and arrange his supplies on the metal table. I turned on a propane heater to give the room just a touch of warmth and then regarded Jeremy with an awkward smile, not really knowing what to say. What could I say? Perhaps, "Well, all ready there, bub?" I think not. There isn't anything appropriate you can say to break the tension before you drug someone and stick them in a cold pine box.

Jeremy folded his arms across his chest. His teeth began to chatter, and I sensed that he was realizing this was by far the *warmest* he was going to be for four months. But his enthusiasm hadn't waned—as soon as William stated, "I'm ready for you, Mr. Clark," he tore off his robe and flipped it to me like I was his butler. Then he hopped up on the rolling bed, leaned back, and took a deep breath.

At last, a taut, nervous expression settled over his face. *I know how you feel, kid. I've been there before.*

Now it was my turn to experience the procedure from the other side.

◉

The only instruction provided to me beforehand by the doctor was simply, "Just follow my lead and give me a helping hand. If I need something, get it for me. Otherwise, I'll handle everything!"

So I stood by, unsure of myself, staring Jeremy directly in his frightened eyes. The vein in his neck twitched and jumped as Dr. Butcher pressed the gas mask over his nose and mouth and quickly released the nitrous oxide. In a soothing voice, the doctor said, "Just breathe normally, Mr. Clark. We're going to count backward from ten. Ten, nine, eight, seven—"

I remembered this part. In fact, it was the *last* thing I remembered about my own procedure. Now I was busy gingerly swabbing Jeremy's forearm with a wad of cotton balls soaked in isopropyl alcohol. William decided it would be best to use his right arm, as it had far fewer scars and needle wounds than the left.

Glancing at Jeremy's face, I saw his eyelids flutter like the beating of a hummingbird's wings while a broad smile stretched from cheekbone to cheekbone, reminiscent of Cesar Romero in full Joker makeup.

"*Hee hee hee . . . .*" he squeaked as he fell into a sedated state. Dr. Butcher and I both chuckled as well. It was a contagious laugh.

"Okay, Daniel, I'm going to decrease the flow of nitrous, but I'd like you to switch places with me and hold down the mask while I administer the pentobarbital. Be sure to keep it pressed snugly over his muzzle, creating an airtight seal. When I instruct you, shut off the gas entirely by turning the knob to the right."

"Sure thing, Will," I said, dropping the cotton swabs into a sap bucket we'd been using as a wastebasket. I circled around and depressed the mask, and the doctor zipped around the foot of the bed, took up the syringe, and sunk the sharp into the patient's forearm with practiced ease. Almost immediately, Jeremy's twitching eyelids became still and his goofy grin vanished as his mouth slowly yawned wide open. His expression reminded me of the Egyptian "screaming mummy" I'd once seen in a photo in a history book.

"Even though he's been clean for a while, I took into account his history of drug abuse and supplied him with a slightly more potent dose than I'd normally administer to a man of his size," explained Dr. Butcher. "I also supplemented it with a trace of morphine, just in case it's needed to keep him out. Looks like he's getting quite a rush."

"You're the doctor, William."

Next, we stripped Jeremy of his gown, leaving him entirely nude—and absurdly vulnerable. I imagined my own body, ghostly white and wrinkly, stretched out like a dead fish on the very same table with the same doctor in attendance.

But there was work to be done and no time to feel shame for events that had taken place twelve months ago.

"Daniel, I am going to outfit the patient with a variety of devices to monitor his pulse, body temperature, and brain activity. Oh, and I need to get the catheter in. While

I'm doing this, I'd like you to finish preparing the casket. Fill the interior compartment with about six inches of water, and then use the bathwater heater and thermometer to raise the temperature to approximately forty-five degrees."

While the doctor painstakingly applied monitors across Jeremy's body, I stood off to the side with my green hose, like a gardener watering a tomato plant. Little time was needed to fill the box with six inches of water, and when that was done, I knelt down with the meat thermometer.

William glanced over at me. "What is the temperature of the tap water?"

"Just a bit over forty-two degrees," I answered.

"Excellent. That will be just about what we will need in a while. Right now though, I need you to raise the temperature to about forty-five degrees."

Repeating himself wasn't necessary, but I kept my mouth shut and switched on the wand-like water heater. After about seven or eight minutes of swishing and swirling the heated tubes around, I achieved the proper temperature.

"Ready here, Will."

"Perfect timing. So am I." He stepped back from the hospital bed, sweat rolling off his forehead, and stripped off his outer layer, a clean, starched white coat. I found it astonishing that he could feel so warm when I was practically shivering, but I understood why when he went over to one of the propane jet heaters and turned it toward the wall.

"Damned thing was cooking me alive, but I didn't want to interrupt you nor myself to move it. Phew! Okay, Dan, it's about time to get this fellow into the water, so while I roll the bed and pole here, I want you to push this over," he said, motioning to the stainless-steel medical table. On each of the two levels of the table sat multiple monitoring devices. Wires sprouted from the monitors and connected to Jeremy's body from forehead to thighs with clamps, bands, and sticky pads. He looked like a cadaver undergoing an elaborate science experiment at the hands of a mad scientist—and that, I thought, wasn't too far from the truth.

It was difficult to look at the kid. The long catheter tube protruding from his crotch made it especially hard not to recoil in discomfort.

"Keep the table close to the bed so nothing comes off," ordered Dr. Butcher. "I don't want to have to reattach any of the affixed monitors. Now, we're going to slide the bed and the table in as close as we can get them to the casket; then, we'll *lift* the patient in unison and *gently* place him in the shallow water. Lastly, you roll the empty bed out of the way. Ready?"

I was, and with the doctor leading the way, we easily moved everything into place. Placing Jeremy into the casket with so many wires and tubes sticking out of his body was challenging, but we did it without giving him any scrapes, bumps, or bruises. Plus, all the monitors and attachments stayed put—even the EEG band, which remained firmly in place as we rested his neck on the shelf that would keep his head elevated above the water line.

"That went much better with you than with Dr. Zargari!" said Butcher with a laugh as I moved the medical table aside. "The weakling dropped you on your head—I'm not sure why I let him carry the shoulders!"

Now, there's information I could have done without.

Running my fingers along the back of my scalp, just above the neck, I touched a small, sore, raised lump of scar tissue that I'd noticed in the past year while washing my hair. It was quite the curiosity, and I could never recall how I'd gotten it. Now I knew.

"Shit, William. That's pretty careless."

"Indeed!" He replied, immediately reverting to his agreeable, upbeat mannerisms to charm the anger out of me. "It was inappropriate of Dr. Zargari to try to lift you when he should have understood his own physical limitations. Fortunately, being in the care of two excellent physicians, the wound was thoroughly cleaned and tightly bandaged. And once we got you in the cold water, the bleeding stopped entirely due to the slowing of your pulse. Speaking of which, I believe you are going to find the steady decrease in heart rate and body temperature of our patient here to be utterly fascinating."

I stood by while Dr. Butcher, kneeling beside the casket, scooped up ladlefuls of water and poured them over Jeremy. Since the pool was so shallow, his body was not yet fully immersed. After more than an hour—perhaps two—had passed, he inserted an IV drip of cool saline.

"It is important to slowly lower the body temperature, both externally and from the inside, so we don't send him into shock—or, worse yet, kill him," the doctor said, now speaking in a grave, quiet voice. "If you watch this screen, you'll see how slowly his core temperature is dropping."

He motioned to a gadget on the lower level of the medical table that resembled a small digital alarm clock. "94.1," it read.

"Still seems very high," I commented.

"Yes, it is. If you touched his skin, you'd never know how much warmth his body still contains."

I lightly stroked Jeremy's shoulder with my fingertips. The doctor was correct. The boy felt like a corpse. His flesh was cool and clammy, slippery and slimy. Not long ago, he was a warm, animate man; now, under our care, he'd been reduced to a spongy, wet, slack-jawed mannequin.

Half of a century had passed since I'd watched my grandma die. Until this point it had been the most horrific thing I'd ever witnessed. But her death, at least, had been natural and total. Death came to free her from her body and unburden her from pain.

But Jeremy? His troubles and pain sat patiently waiting for this quasi-death to end. He would awaken in a few months the same broken human. I hadn't defused a bomb—I'd just added a small amount of time to the ticker.

Dr. Butcher and I were merchants of false hope and artificial serenity.

At that moment, if I weren't a coward, I would have

done whatever it took to free Jeremy. I would have called off the whole thing, and I'd have beaten the doctor with my fists if he'd resisted. I would have found a way to return the thousands of dollars we'd accepted from the other four patients, and I would have found them help—*real* help, not the fake promises we offered by dangling their lives over the precipice of death.

But I was, am, and always have been a coward. At that moment I felt intimidated by the doctor and even more afraid that if I had to use force against him, I wouldn't be able to revive Jeremy safely on my own.

More time crawled by. Dr. Butcher provided Jeremy with his first shot of DPCPX; I was amazed he found an available spot on the body to stick a needle. Even heavily drugged, the comatose boy shivered and took deep breaths. After a while, the quivering stopped and his breathing slowed.

"Now it is time to add more water to the casket," the doctor said at long last. "Squeeze the nozzle just hard enough to let out a gentle stream. The basin will fill slowly. And be careful not to spray above the neck, as we want to keep our patient's head perfectly dry."

Gradually, the water drizzled out. Every time I looked at the monitors, I could see the number representing body temperature falling and the electrocardiogram tracing continuously slowing. If I'd been connected to the machine, my own EKG reading would have been through the roof. I trembled, afraid of what I was doing, struggling to steady the nozzle of the garden hose.

Dr. Butcher stood by, giving his full attention to Jeremy and the medical readings. He said nothing for forty-five minutes except for the occasional, "Yes, good," muttered in a half-whisper.

Suddenly, just as the water level had nearly reached the fill-line, Jeremy's body twitched as he sucked in a huge gulp of air; a shrill, strained noise emanated from his throat, sounding much like the dying breath of my grandmother.

"Oh, shit, he's going to die!" I shouted as the hose fell to the floor. The handle of the nozzle hit the ground and sent a spurt of water straight up, soaking the crotch and right leg of my jeans. I took a step toward the side of the casket, but the doctor threw out his arm and blocked me just before I could reach in and pull Jeremy out to revive him.

"No, he's fine, he's *fine!*" yelled Dr. Butcher. "The body is naturally reacting to the massive changes it is going through—*you* reacted the same way!"

I paused and looked him in his eyes. His brow was knitted with anger, and he glared at me coldly.

"If you take him out now, the shock could kill him. You need to have *trust* in me and understand that *I* am the professional here—not you! If I deem him to be in any danger, I will take appropriate action. Understood?"

"Yes," I said, stunned at the outburst. "I understand."

He'd put me in my place. I was a foolish child; the doctor was master.

Dr. Butcher gave Jeremy a small dose of phenobarbital, which calmed the spasms. Then we finished filling the casket in silence. Dr. Butcher returned to his monitors and gadgets, and I to my hose.

◉

Finally, in the early afternoon, Dr. Butcher announced that torpor had been successfully induced. The water temperature was a suitable 39.9 degrees, which had been achieved by adding a small amount of ice directly to the water in which Jeremy lay. All vital signs were normal, at least, considering the situation.

"Couple questions, Will," I said. "Don't we need to fill the outer compartment of the casket with ice to maintain the temperature of the inner compartment?"

"Excellent question," he said. His famous sunny disposition had returned. "When we put you under, Dr. Zargari and I quickly learned that as long as the outdoor temperature stayed below forty degrees, it was not necessary to add ice to either compartment. In fact, it was *so* cold that we had to keep the propane heaters running throughout most of January and February just to keep you from becoming encased in ice yourself! No, we need only add ice to the outer compartment during warmer days, generally in late winter when the temperatures occasionally climb above forty." He cleared his throat. "What is your other question?"

"Well, I was just wondering why Jeremy's eyes are partway open."

"It is a bit 'chilling,' no?" He laughed out loud. "I know that it is a bit off-putting, but it is natural for the eyelids to open partway when the body has entered a state of such relaxation. The muscles that hold your eyes shut during sleep are not fully functioning. Therefore, it is important for eye drops to be administered at least once every few hours," he said, plucking a small dropper from the mess atop the medical table. "Regular contact lens saline is fine. We used it on you, and as I recall, your vision returned to normal within several hours of awakening."

"Yeah," I said. "I don't remember. I can see fine now."

We retreated to the house for a late lunch. After the meal, the doctor announced that he'd spend the rest of the day and the entire night by Jeremy's side. "I like to spend the first night with the patient, just to ensure that everything is fine."

"Good. It makes me feel good to know you're taking such good care of him, William," I said.

"Absolutely! And by the way, tomorrow morning, I'll need to borrow your truck, as I need to retrieve four more medical tables and IV poles."

"You got it, Will. Keys are hanging on the hook by the front door. If I'm sleeping, no need to wake me."

I stayed in the house for the rest of the day and night. I was worn down, my emotions spent. I could think of nothing I'd rather do than rest on the couch and forget about everything we'd just done to that half-dead boy in my sugar shack.

◉

Two days later, Lauren Andrews of New Haven, Connecticut arrived. She was followed by Kevin Christopher, fifty-two, of Las Vegas, and Rebecka Pollard, the medical student from Lake Forest, California. Andrews and Christopher accepted treatment easily, with no resistance. Neither engaged in any conversation, nor did they display much emotion beyond wan indifference.

Pollard was a different story. The moment the girl entered the cold sugarhouse and saw the sheets draped over the hibernating bodies, she broke down in tears. She was a pretty young thing from sun-drenched Southern California. Now, after dropping a small fortune for the privilege, she'd ended up practically naked in a frigid shack in the gloomy Vermont woods with two strange old men, thousands of miles from home. I wanted to weep along with her.

But you could never doubt the soothing, persuasive manner of Dr. Butcher. Somehow, he cajoled the hysterical girl to crawl up onto the hospital bed and lean back. She whimpered and squirmed as tears cascaded from the corners of her eyes and into her ears. And just as she screamed, "*I can't do this! I want to go home!*" Butcher snuck the gas mask over her face and fully opened the nitrous tank. She took a single deep breath and was out cold in seconds.

"Poor girl!" said Dr. Butcher with a sympathetic laugh, shaking his head. "Did she really think she had a choice at this point?"

21.

I can't recall a day I've dreaded as much as December 13, 1994. Call it a hunch; call it a premonition; call it whatever you want. I had a horrible feeling about Joe Gooley, and I didn't get a wink of sleep the night before our fifth and final subject arrived for treatment.

The thing is, whether you sleep or not, morning always arrives. Giving in to anxiety and insomnia can only make the following day worse, so you might as well get a good night's sleep. Better to face your dread fresh-faced and perky than groggy and grumpy. That's always been my belief.

But beliefs can't comfort a troubled mind and rock you to sleep. After tossing in bed for ninety minutes, I got up, went to the liquor cabinet, and threw back a shot and a half of bourbon to calm my nerves, shuddering as it scorched my tongue and smoldered in my belly. Then, after cramming the firebox full of well-seasoned ash logs,

I settled into a wicker rocking chair in the basement by the woodstove to relax with a book. The dim lighting and the soothing dry heat suggested that I'd be whisked off to dreamland in no time.

But the book was no good. I tossed it aside. Plus, the blazing waves of heat rolling off the surface of the cast iron woodstove were suffocating me. Perspiring, I arose and paced the hallways and stomped up and down three flights of stairs, back and forth, sweating even more and growing exhausted. Still, my tired body resisted the allure of slumber. I drank a few beers around four a.m. to enjoy the buzz, and when it became apparent that I just wasn't going to doze off, I put on a pot of coffee.

I finished my fifth cup around quarter to seven—right when I began to feel sleep coming on in spite of my racing heart. But it was too late for rest. My guts rumbled from the nasty cocktail of booze and black coffee I'd poured down my gullet, and I hustled off to the bathroom for a nasty bout of diarrhea, a long shower, and a quick shave. The shower lasted so long I emptied the hot water tank and had to run my razor under the cold spigot.

After spending nearly an hour in the bathroom, I dressed myself in layers, choked down a piece of white toast, and welcomed the subzero air, the morning sun, and our final guest with bleary, bloodshot eyes.

◉

Mr. Gooley arrived with Dr. Butcher at eight o'clock on the button. I had to hand it to William—he was always promptly on time. And I appreciated it, as I'd been waiting for them on the porch since I really didn't want to invite Joe into my house again. Up in the sugar shack, I'd already concealed all the bodies beneath thin cotton sheets and had set up the medical table with all the instruments I knew the doctor would need. By now we had a set, familiar routine.

The car came to a stop, and Dr. Butcher killed the engine. Before the thick, white cloud of car exhaust that had poured from the tailpipe could dissipate, the doctor stepped out of his car and slammed the door shut. With an attitude as chilly as the weather, he briskly circled around the car without saying a word or acknowledging Joseph or me. Instead, he stomped up along the side of the house and beat a path straight to the sugar shack.

Accustomed to this type of off-putting treatment, Joe slowly pulled himself out of the Oldsmobile and wordlessly greeted me with a single nod. I returned the nod and saw that he was already dressed in the hospital gown, with only a pair of boxer shorts beneath it and a shabby pair of bedroom slippers on his feet.

"You could have changed here," I said.

"Doc tol' me to get changed at home," he said. "He tol' me I wouldn't need no other clothes."

"Where are your glasses?"

"Left 'em at home also," he replied.

"I would like to get this procedure underway, please," Dr. Butcher shouted flatly from off in the distance. From the sound of his voice he had nearly reached the shack.

"All right," I muttered, already weary of the doctor. Then, looking at Joe, I said, "Follow me."

During the walk to the outbuilding, I glanced back repeatedly at my old childhood classmate, assessing his size. Unlike the other patients, who'd arrived plump and loaded with ample body fat to sustain them throughout the long winter, Gooley looked hardly any heavier than the last time I'd seen him. In fact, I wasn't sure whether he'd put on any weight at all.

Of course, when I'd awoken from my hibernation, I'd found that I'd lost very little weight—barely fifteen pounds, if I remembered correctly. I'd needed to exercise vigorously just to *lose* the excess pounds packed on prior to my deep sleep. So maybe, I thought, Dr. Butcher had overstated the importance of putting on extra weight all along. A leaner fellow like Joe might benefit from a less stout physique.

His stringy gray hair and nappy, tangled beard, however, had certainly grown longer and bushier since we'd last met. He looked like a dirty, vagrant drunk stumbling across the icy field, sliding and nearly tumbling the entire way. Only as we approached the door did I finally offer him a hand.

"Thanks," he said, teeth chattering. "No treads on my slippers. Think I'd be better off wearin' nothin' at all."

I swung open the door to the sugar shack and held it for Joe to enter. He shuffled inside, dragging his feet on the floor.

"Get inside and shut the door," commanded Dr. Butcher. "We've got to maintain a consistent temperature in here."

But if Joe had heard him, he didn't let on. Slowly, he entered the building, squinting and looking around with the overwhelming awe of a young child on Christmas morning. His chapped lips formed an "O" shape beneath the bushel of white facial hair as he took in the sights and sounds of medical monitors and shrouded bodies in a room meant for making syrup.

There was one empty casket. And beside it stood Dr. Butcher.

"Slip off your shorts and gown and get in," he said, pointing at it.

Shaking with cold, Gooley started toward the doctor. Then he paused and looked back and forth between the two of us with tight lips and misty, blinking eyes. He bunched up the fabric of his gown in his two liver-spotted fists and said, quietly, "Just wanna thank you both for doin' this for me. First good thing anyone's done for me in a long, long time."

Stunned, William and I looked at each other. Finally, the doctor simply said, "You paid us. Now get in the box."

"You're welcome," I added. But Joe had already turned his back to me and was sliding off his shorts at the foot of the casket.

Hold on, now. The doctor just told him to get in the casket.

Every person we'd treated so far had started out on the medical table in the center of the room so that Dr. Butcher could anesthetize the patient and properly apply monitoring equipment. Why now was he hustling Joe into the casket?

"William," I said.

"Please, Mr. Fassett, call me 'Dr. Butcher' in front of the patient," he cut in.

"Fine, *Doctor*—would you like me to get the hospital bed?"

Joe, indifferent to it all and not knowing any better, dropped his gown to the floor. Naked, he stepped into the shallow water and simply said, "Hmm. That's cold."

Dr. Butcher nodded at Joseph, motioning for him to lie down, and then returned his attention to me. "It's not needed. I will be able to affix all the monitors and insert the catheter prior to the complete submersion of Mr. Gooley."

"But . . . the cold," I said.

"It's my opinion that we've been wasting valuable time by starting the patient out on the bed—not to mention inconveniencing ourselves by having to transfer them to the casket." He got down on his knees just as Joe settled his head and neck onto the elevated shelf. "Mr. Gooley won't be aware of anything once he is sedated."

And with that, without warning, he depressed the gas mask over Joe's face and turned the crank.

"Take a deep breath."

Joe took two breaths and immediately relaxed. The nitrous-induced grin I'd grown so familiar with in the past week spread over his face, and he began to laugh.

"Hee hee heeee . . . ."

Still, it seemed to me that the doctor had supplied a light dose in comparison to those he'd provided the other patients. But maybe, I thought, it was just my impression.

Now it was time to inject the barbiturate anesthetic. Instead, the doctor hastily began to stick body temperature and cardiac monitor pads onto Gooley's body.

"Hee hee," said Joe, moving his arms and fidgeting about in the freezing bath the doctor had prepared for him.

Like an impatient parent bathing a toddler, the doctor snapped, "Be still!" Then he leaned into Joe and drove his elbow into the nest of wiry silver hairs on his bony chest, pinning him down.

I cleared my throat. "Correct me if I'm mistaken, *Doctor*, but I'm sure this is where you give the intravenous anesthetic."

"Unfortunately, I cannot," he said, not turning to face me. "My supply ran out, and I've not been able to procure any more pentobarbital."

"How could you not have any access to medication?"

"Because barbiturates are heavily regulated, difficult to obtain, and *costly*." He spoke swiftly, impatiently. "I will be injecting the DPCPX shortly, and I have plenty of phenobarbital on hand—which, to remind you, is the drug used throughout the procedure to ensure a constant state of torpor. Now, if you don't mind, I need to concentrate."

He snapped the pulse oximeter over Joe's left pointer finger, then placed the EEG band around his forehead, grimacing in visible disgust at having to touch the man's hairline.

Can't wait to see how he acts when it comes time to place the catheter.

Joe lifted his head, grinning and laughing like a hyena. Despite his nitrous-induced state of hysterical intoxication, I could see that he was uncomfortable and wanted to escape. But the doctor caught him by his trembling forehead and slammed his skull back down hard into the wood.

"William—"

"*Doctor,*" he said, again correcting me.

"No, *William*, goddamnit! The patient doesn't know any better at this point what I call you! Now, let's keep in mind that this man paid nearly a full *third* of the money you've brought in and is funding a large part of—"

"First of all, it is money that *we* have brought in, Daniel!" He jumped to his feet, surprising me with this dexterity, and wagged a finger as he spoke. "We are *business* partners in this, let's not forget. But I am going to remind you, once and for all, that *I* am the medical professional, not you. I hold this man's safety in the highest regard, in spite of his . . . *disgusting* history!"

"Not your place to be judging right now, Will. It's time to do your job."

"I *am* doing my job, and I will continue to do it how I see fit," he said, preparing the shot of DPCPX. He sighed deeply. "The cost overruns here have exceeded my expectations, and our profit will be disappointingly marginal this winter. Here, with our final patient, we have a perfect specimen to test the efficacy and safety of more rapid induction of torpor."

The doctor returned to his knees to give Gooley the shot. The DPCPX relaxed him a bit. Not entirely, but his movements slowed considerably.

"Now, please, do not worry. And do *not* bother me! This man will be fine—but I need to be allowed to concentrate, and I need to be able to work in peace and without having my methods incessantly questioned."

It felt colder than normal in the sugar shack, but sweat glistened on Dr. Butcher's forehead below his thick white hair. He dabbed his face with a tissue and removed his wire-rimmed glasses to wipe clean the lenses. Then he picked up the garden hose, which sat on the floor just to his left, and began to fill the casket.

"Help me out here by holding him down," Dr. Butcher said.

"*Hee hee hee*," Gooley said.

◉

I thought the DPCPX would take effect quickly, but it did not. I thought that hypothermia and all the physical comfort it offers would settle in quickly, but it did not. I thought Joe would go into shock.

He did not. At least, I don't believe he did.

But he did suffer. I know, because witnessing his drugged, panicked face contorting in the ice-cold water reminded me of how I must have looked in the river during my accident two years prior.

I had it easy by comparison. In December, the Mad River reaches temperatures around freezing—but the water from my garden hose was warmer by ten full degrees. It makes a difference.

"The bastard just won't enter the torpor phase," said an incredulous Dr. Butcher after forty-five minutes of lightly soaking Gooley. "I'll have to take note of this. I never realized the massive importance of the initial dose of pentobarbital. It really is interesting." He scooped up ice chips with the metal ladle and dumped them into the water.

Rage boiled my blood, and I could feel my neck flush and redden. I wanted to let go of Gooley and wrap my frigid fingers around William's neck. But I was culpable as well. I'd gotten myself in way over my head, and I had to point the finger of blame at myself too.

Never in my life had I desired to stand over anyone—convicted pedophile or not—and hold them down in a tub of cold water. But here I was, doing it of my own free will, lackey to a madman. My fingers ached to the bone, as if I'd plunged them into a snow bank. How must Gooley feel?

Finally, I asked, "What about the other one? The other anesthetic. The phenobarbital. Use that."

"Not yet," he said. "I'm afraid that in his current state, it might cause his blood pressure to drop too rapidly."

I'd been staring at Joe for what felt like days, moving my hands around to restrain him every time he tried to move. If he lifted a leg, I pressed it down. If he attempted to raise his shoulders, I pushed them back. The whole time he stared at me, eyes half-open and glazed, the nitrous grin slow to fade from his scraggly mug.

We made eye contact. I wondered if he could still see me, and if he could, what he thought of me at that moment.

Suddenly, Gooley began to twitch and shudder violently. His legs kicked up and straightened out, entirely out of the water below the knees, and both arms flailed, splashing water across the doctor's coat as he tended his monitors. Then a half-closed fist flew out, wrinkled and pale, and socked me in the mouth. I felt less like I'd been punched and more like my jaw had been smacked with a wet snowball. Water sloshed up over the edges of the casket's inner layer and ran down the sides into the outer compartments.

By this point, I was accustomed to patient spasms. But this? Nothing else had come close to it all week.

"Hold him down! *Hold him down!*" yelled Dr. Butcher, his glasses spattered with water droplets. He scrambled to locate a hypodermic needle and a syringe, fumbling with monitors and wires. Then he spun and knocked the IV pole on its side. The catheter bag fell to the floor, and the bag of cooling saline, still being fed into a vein in Gooley's forearm, burst as it hit the plywood. The doctor shoved me out of the way, shouting, "Move!" before plunging the tip of the needle into Gooley's neck and emptying the contents of the syringe.

The thrashing stopped, and Gooley settled back into place. His eyelids slowly shut. The insane smile vanished from his face as his jaw went slack. Peace at last.

In the aftermath of the horrific display, the doctor and I stood facing each other, both straining to catch our breath. We both were disheveled and soaked. Then the doctor reviewed the readings on each monitor and piped up.

"It looks like we've just about done it, Daniel! Mr. Gooley's vitals appear to be normal, and I'd say that within an hour or so, I'll have his body temperature consistent with that of the other patients. This means we'll have induced hibernation in less than one-third of the time the others required! Missteps aside, I'd say we were quite successful, and I've certainly learned a lot that we can apply to future procedures."

I couldn't believe it. Just like that, Mr. Hyde had stepped out, and amiable Dr. Jekyll had returned, as if nothing were unusual. I stared blankly, blinking and wordless.

He wiped his hands on his jacket and looked around. "I think I have quite a mess to pick up here. Plus, we are overdue to check on the other patients." He put a hand on his hip. "Tell you what," he said, clapping my shoulder like the old friend he once had been, "why don't you go inside and rest? I will have to skip lunch, but I'll be sure to fill up at dinner. I have a long night ahead of me!"

22.

More often than not, I spent my nights sleeping on the living room couch. It wasn't a recently developed habit, but something I'd begun doing long ago, when Sandy left me. Years later, on some nights, I still reached out to wrap her in my arms as I fell asleep in our lonely queen-sized bed. But on the couch, where I could stare at the television until my eyes gave out, there was space only for me. Plus, in the wintertime, it was warmer there. Closer to the roaring woodstove in the cellar and the residual heat from the oven in the kitchen.

But with Dr. Butcher slinking around my house lately, I'd taken to retiring to my bedroom almost every evening. After the debacle with Joseph Gooley, I had no desire to see him, today or on any other day. I knew I'd have to face him again, but I was weak and sick with fear and worry. A long night of catatonic sleep was desperately needed. I retreated to my bedroom at six o'clock.

I read in bed by the light of an antique kerosene lamp Sandy and I received from her parents on our wedding day. I nodded and skimmed the words on the pages for several hours, finally falling into a deep slumber shortly after nine.

◉

At a few minutes past four in the morning, I awoke. The heavy-lidded sluggishness I'd felt upon falling asleep was gone; now, I was wide awake immediately upon opening my eyes.

A beam of moonlight poured in at a sharp angle through the six-pane window, leaving the shadow of a grid on the wooden floor. There was no other light, as the lamp had burned through all the oil in the reservoir. My book had fallen to the floor.

I'd been so tired that I hadn't bothered to undress, nor had I even crawled beneath the covers. I terribly needed to go to the bathroom, so I swung my legs over the side of the bed and tiptoed down the creaky stairs. No, tiptoeing was not necessary, but the habit I'd acquired from living for so many years with a wife and children had never left me.

The only bathroom in the house was on the first floor. That was an unfortunate part of living in an ancient farmhouse, constructed long before the advent of indoor plumbing. Just one more advantage to sleeping on the couch, steps away from the lone toilet.

I flushed the john, and instead of retreating to my bedroom, I entered the kitchen. Walking around the cold house had awoken me further, and after seven solid hours of sleep, I was feeling quite rested. Not to mention, the longer I stayed awake, the more time I had to reminisce on the appalling events of the previous day.

I clicked on the fluorescent tube lamp over the kitchen sink, filled my teapot, and lit a burner on the stove. Somewhere in the house, I was sure to have a bag of chamomile. Mixed with a spoonful of honey and a drop of milk, it would surely relax me enough to send me back to bed for a couple more hours. At least, it would be a better option than the combination of whiskey and beer I'd stupidly downed the previous night. I had to shake my head when I thought about the booze-bomb I'd dropped on my unsuspecting guts.

Far in the back of the kitchen cupboard I found a pale-yellow box of tea.

Chamomile. Perfect.

The teapot began to whistle like a steam train, so I dropped a teabag into my mug and filled it to the brim with boiling water. I continued to shuffle around the house while it steeped, trying to keep my mind off of the sugar shack and my collection of frozen bodies, tended to by a man I truly wished I'd never have to see again.

But I couldn't get them off my mind. Despite not wanting to look, I casually drifted into the mudroom and put my face against the glass window in the back door, looking up the gentle slope of the backyard toward the shack.

The door of the sugar shack was closed, but I could see light pouring out from under it, illuminating a thin strip of snow. And even with the thick, dark blankets draped over the painted windows, the glow from the ring of work lamps leaked through, just a bit.

I backed away from the window. My heart raced and my breathing had steadily grown heavy. I looked down at my hands and realized they trembled uncontrollably.

I can't go on like this. I cannot spend the next four months like this.

I certainly didn't know how to broach the subject to Dr. Butcher, but he'd have to know how I felt, and soon. He might not take it well, but at this point, I didn't care what he thought. He may have spent a great deal out of pocket, but the sugar shack was *my* damned property, and he couldn't force me to allow him access to *my* property.

Whatever he'd spent, I'd reimburse him. I'd pay him back no matter how long it took—no matter how deeply it plunged me into poverty. I'd cut him in for half my pension checks until he was paid back in full. Whatever it took, I'd do it.

In the morning. I'll tell him in the morning.

But that narrow band of yellow light along the bottom of the sugar shack door was drawing me toward it like a moth to a candle flame. Even if I didn't mention my plans to end our partnership, I had to go up there. If I didn't, I wouldn't be able to put it out of my mind. If the light was on, the doctor was likely still awake. And if he'd passed out on the old Army cot in the back corner, I'd switch off the lights and let him rest alongside everyone else.

I popped my boots on over my socks and put on a beat-up, checkered wool hunting jacket as I walked back toward the kitchen. My cup of tea was blistering hot. I took a small sip and placed it back on the light-blue laminate countertop to cool. In ten minutes or so, it would be just the right temperature.

◉

It was a crystal-clear night. Sunrise was coming soon, but with the moon sinking on the horizon, a handful of stars twinkled overhead, if only for a moment before the light of dawn erased them from the sky. It was beautiful, brutally cold, and completely hushed except for the muffled sound of crusty snow crunching beneath my feet.

The door of the sugarhouse could only be locked from the outside, but its considerable weight held it shut securely even without a latch. As quietly as possible, I slowly swung open the heavy door and peeked in, expecting to see the exhausted doctor passed out from the long day and endless night spent in the cold confines of the shack.

A hinge creaked slightly as I poked my head in. The cot was vacant except for a rumpled wool blanket and a lumpy pillow. And William, to my surprise, was wide awake, standing beside Joe Gooley. With an expression of guilt and surprise, the old doctor stared at me open-mouthed.

Finally, he spoke. "What are you doing here now? Get out!"

What I saw made me want to obey. But I couldn't tear my eyes away from the horrific sight.

On the IV pole hung two bags I recognized from before. One was the empty bag of saline, which had exploded when it fell to the floor; the other was the catheter bag, containing only a slight amount of dark-yellow urine.

However, a new bag hung with the others on a lower hook: a larger bag, receiving a slow stream of thick, dark crimson. Atop the steel medical table sat a bizarre contraption resembling a small electric kitchen blender. It made a soft whirring noise as it drew blood up through a tube connected intravenously to Gooley's leg. The blood passed through the vacuum pump chamber and into a second tube, which fed the large, clear IV bag.

At first, I could not make sense of what I'd stumbled upon. Despite Dr. Butcher's cruel tactics and harsh manner in the past week, I'd never expected to find him, a beloved small-town family practitioner for half a century, performing such a warped, evil experiment on a human with a beating heart.

It looked as though Gooley were being embalmed alive. Yet despite the outflow of blood, there were no fluids being pumped *into* the man.

At last, I found my voice. "What are you doing? What are you *doing to Gooley*, William?"

He stuttered only for a moment. Then he began to work his golden-tongued magic.

"I certainly wasn't expecting you to show up here in the early hours of the morning, Daniel. Truth be told, I was hoping to have a few full nights in private to smooth out all the potential wrinkles in my new procedure. But since you are here and have already taken in an eyeful, I may as well fully disclose everything, so that you aren't left with any bad impressions!"

"Will, I'm not too sure I could have any worse of an impression right now," I said, trying to keep my voice steady.

"I understand, believe me. I know it looks awful!" He forced a laugh and took a step toward me. I stepped back and he halted, motioning to the odd device on the medical table.

"This here is a small embalming pump. It's got a few years on it, but you'll be happy to know that it has been fully tested and sterilized in advance, and it works like a charm. Now, normally, to extract blood from a patient, one needs only to insert a needle and allow the heart to do all the work, pumping blood through the tubing and into the collection bag. *However*, due to the slowed heart rate of the chilled specimen here, obtaining blood requires some assistance from this machine. It is perfectly safe and uses centrifugal force to create a suction that draws the blood from the body. Now, I've set it to a very low setting, and the blood draw is going much more slowly than it would if he simply had a normal pulse—"

"*William!*" I shouted, pointing at him as I advanced. "Why the *fuck* are you taking blood from Gooley in the first place?"

He took a step back and put up his hands, palms toward me, as if to ward off my anger. "Well, Daniel, that—that is the other thing I need to explain to you. And again, I truly believe that despite your fears, you will agree that what I am working toward is a very noble cause. I really think—"

I stopped my advancement. "Explain."

He cleared his throat. "Daniel, we have already—largely, I must emphasize, thanks to your visionary idea—broken ground on an incredible therapeutic treatment that has the capability to benefit thousands upon thousands of people. However, the induced hibernation aspect of this procedure is not our endgame. No, it is, in fact, the tip of the iceberg."

I looked at the bag of blood. A slow, deep-red trickle continued to stream into it.

"Across the Earth, Daniel, emergency blood supplies are never—and likely never will be—completely full. As long as there are humans, there will always be tragedy and disease. And with that knowledge, there will always be a need for blood of all types.

"There is more than enough blood to go around," he continued, "but not enough people are willing to go out of their way to give it. Illegal blood farms have cropped up around the globe, often in places desperate for an adequate supply."

"So you wanted to get in on the action?" I asked.

"Don't insult me!" the doctor shouted. "In actuality, I am hoping to offer an alternative source for regions in dire need of fresh blood."

"Then join the Red Cross."

"The Red Cross," he said with an amused expression, "only *wishes* they had the resources I have."

"I hardly believe that. You've got five people here in a backwoods shack. That's not what I'd consider a large supply."

"No, it's not," he said, nodding in agreement. "Far from it. But trust me when I say I have resources, Daniel."

"You don't have shit," I said, challenging his cocky proclamation. "You're an old crackpot doctor in the boondocks."

"You don't live as long as I do and have a profession like mine without making a few connections," he said, correcting me. "My plan isn't to make a fortune now off of these people. Now I am merely in the preliminary testing phase—seeing what works, what doesn't. But once that is done, with the support of a friend, I will soon have more sources of fresh, safe blood than I can handle."

"Your friend?"

"Yes, my friend. The warden of one of the state's largest prisons. Together we can fund the construction of a building large enough to hold hundreds of prisoners. He'll get to relieve crowding in his cells, and the prisoners will have the opportunity to give back to a world they've taken so much from—whether they like it or not."

The doctor, becoming incensed, pointed at Gooley and kicked the heavy wooden casket with the toe of his boot. "Why should the worst *shit* humanity has to offer, like this wretched child-raping asshole, get to hoard one of the most precious resources on Earth? In time, we will be able to offer our hibernation services to prisons across the continent! Blood shortages will be eliminated, and at long last, criminals will truly be able to pay their debts to society. Capital punishment advocates say that if you take a life, then you should lose *your* life. How about instead, if you take a life, you *save countless lives*? It's ethical, it's safe—and it will be *massively* profitable!"

He was raving. I could hardly speak.

"This is madness," I said quietly. "William, unhook Joe from that machine and get off my property. You're no longer welcome here. I'm going to call the hospital and request help to revive these people."

I backed away and turned to open the door. As soon as I took my eyes off Dr. Butcher, he reached for something inside his jacket and I heard a loud click.

He held out a .22 mini-revolver and leveled it at my head.

"Stop right there. Trust me, Daniel. You don't want this to end for you like it did for Dr. Zargari."

23.

I froze by the open door, weighing my options. If I stayed put, he might shoot me. Maybe not, if I cooperated. If I ran . . . there was a chance I could flee the building before he pulled the trigger. But even if I got out of the sugar shack alive, it was a long dash to my house, with few places to hide in between.

Dr. Butcher did not move. He stood stock-still and wild-eyed, with a level arm that kept the gun aimed true—right between my eyes.

Then he spoke in a loud, booming voice. "It is beyond me, Daniel, how you *and* Dr. Zargari could object so strongly to an idea that would have benefited both you and the world so greatly. The blood we could harvest would save countless lives. It would provide a sense of justice to the world. And it would provide you with all the income you could ever need for the rest of your life. Do you want that dream house in Key Largo, Daniel? You could have it. Want to give your children and grandchildren the comfort they deserve? You could. For Christ's sake, Daniel, there are *no victims* here beyond those who deserve to be victimized."

This turn of events had shaken me to the core. Having my lifelong family practitioner threatening to blow my head off in my backyard was inconceivable—yet it was happening.

"You killed Dr. Zargari," is all I could manage, my voice trailing off.

"Yes," he answered point-blank. "Yes, I did. I had to. When I first approached him with this idea, late last February, he was horrified. Simply *horrified*. After he vehemently objected, I laughed it off, played it as if I had been joking. And it got me to thinking: Perhaps I *was* in the wrong. Perhaps his moral objection was justified, and I should give my plans a second thought. And I did. But no matter how hard I thought on it, I couldn't agree with him. No, this is the opportunity of a lifetime. It is a chance to change the world for the better and to be remembered for all time for my contributions to medicine.

"So, after much contemplation, I decided to proceed with my plans. But I was deeply bothered by Dr. Zargari's reaction and very worried that he might tell somebody. After all, as you said, I'm just a family doctor 'in a backwoods town.' Zargari, however, worked in Burlington for as long as I'd been here in Granbury. He knew every medical professional in the state and beyond—not to mention, many people in law enforcement. I felt paranoid and vulnerable. So I began to carry *this* little beauty." He rotated the gun in his hand, never once shifting the aim away from my face.

"Zargari, God bless him, never once mentioned what I'd confided in him to anyone else," continued Dr. Butcher, "but he *did* stumble upon my *first* attempt at the experiment about nine months ago, in March. Showed up from Burlington on a day he wasn't scheduled to be here. Much the same way you showed up here tonight. Just my luck!"

"So that means that—"

"Yes, Daniel, you were the first to have your blood drawn."

Apparently, being dropped on my head wasn't the worst crime that had been committed against me during my time in the two doctors' care.

"I only drew your blood once, however, and thanks to Dr. Zargari, I was not able to accomplish much. I'd like to have continued my research on you. But once I dispatched the doctor, created an autopsy report, and had his remains cremated, I was short on time and knew I'd need assistance to revive you. Your children had to be contacted, and I realized that, unfortunately, I'd have to wait until this winter to continue my experiment in earnest. But I needed people to test on, which is why I leaked the story to the press. I knew that *somewhere* out there, volunteers would be willing to put their bodies in my hands. Who knew we'd have the perfect candidate right in our own backyard? Mr. Gooley here represents every low-life criminal who is going to flood the world with valuable, life-giving blood.

"And please, Daniel, understand that the experiment on you caused no harm. I had nothing but the utmost respect for you and will remain, to my death, ever grateful for the opportunities you have given me. When I say I owe this all to you, I truly mean it. It pains me deeply that I'm going to have to—"

I'd heard enough. I turned and ran out the door and bolted left. The explosion of the gunshot rang out from inside the sugar shack.

Dr. Butcher did not shout or call after me. He didn't need to—I knew that he was right on my heels as I sprinted, leaping like a white-tailed deer, across the snowy field, bluish-gray in the earliest light of morning. However, fast as Butcher might have been, I also knew that he would have to stop, aim, and try to get off a clean shot in the dim morning while I moved farther away from him.

Crack! A second shot. I heard a bullet whiz through the branches of the apple tree as I scuttled beneath its lowest limbs.

I only need a couple seconds more. Almost to the back door. Almost there—

The back entrance door to the house, leading into the mudroom, was practically in reach. Once inside, I could barricade the doors and phone the police. But as I extended my hand to grasp the door knob, a bullet hissed by my ear and shattered the window of the door.

A small burst of glass shards rained down before my feet.

There simply wasn't enough time for me to open the door, get inside, lock it, and barricade it. I darted to my left and ran along the side of the house. I had no plan as to what to do next—and I'd just opened myself up for a clear shot.

Dr. Butcher fired again, and the bullet buried itself in a clapboard. So far, he was zero for three—but I could feel my luck running out.

As I circled around the front of the house, I glanced over my shoulder. The doctor was barely a hundred feet behind me, running with the gun pointed at the sky. And he was gaining on me. I couldn't believe the shape he was in. I'd been running religiously for months, and yet it was likely that he would have been able to beat me in both a fifty-yard dash and a cross-country race.

I crossed Old Stage Road, nearly tripping before jumping off the far side and vaulting over the culvert. I landed atop a rock-hard snow bank and tumbled headfirst, breaking through a hard layer of ice.

Crack! Another shot. A bullet sang as it flew over my head and continued on its way into the woods at the far end of Sandy's meadow. If I hadn't tripped, I might have caught the slug right between the shoulder blades.

I scrambled to my feet and darted toward the gigantic, ancient barn on Sandy's property.

He must be getting short on bullets. But if I enter the barn, it might allow Butcher to corner me.

Afraid of trapping myself, I chose to merely circle the barn and then flee through the small field toward Sandy's house. If the doctor lost sight of me, perhaps I could sneak into Sandy's place to use her telephone. It was a long shot, but I might have a chance. *If only the snow didn't give away my tracks!*

Crack!

This time, the doctor's aim was true. A slug tore into the right side of my back, breaking through my ribcage and burying itself in my lung. I landed on all fours, gasping, and coughed up bright blobs of blood. It splattered the crust of the snow between my hands, a beautiful contrast of rich crimson on pale white.

Behind me, stomping through the rime, Dr. Butcher approached. He wheezed and gasped for oxygen, likely glad that he'd run down his prey and the pursuit had ended. Whether he had any bullets left in his revolver, I could not be sure—but what was certain was that he aimed to kill me. Somehow, he would find a way. I had to admit, after the chase I'd given him, he'd earned it.

I wasn't afraid. Frankly, I was relieved. It was my time; in fact, it had *been* my time a couple years earlier when I'd crashed into the Mad River. It was only by sheer luck that I had been spotted and then pulled to safety by the faceless passersby whose names I'd never learned. Funny that he and I had both saved a life—and because of that, other lives had been needlessly ruined.

Bring it on, Dr. Butcher. Do whatever it is that you have to do.

My vision was hazy and my arms were weak, threatening to give out. Clots of blood and saliva flowed from my lower lip and puddled in the snow.

Boom!

A final gunshot rang out, echoing over the silent treetops. However, it was much louder than the pops from Dr. Butcher's .22.

Plus, I was still alive.

And then I heard the doctor's body flop over and land in a heap of flesh and fabric in the snow. Still positioned on all fours, I slowly craned my neck to look back.

Sure enough, the doctor had been taken out. The left half of Butcher's skull had been blown to bits, and a cascade of purplish fluid and gray matter gushed from the fresh fatal wound over what little remained of his face.

Then I looked up in the direction of Sandy's house. There she was, running toward me, a blurry vision sprinting barefoot through the white pasture in the blue morning. Her silver hair hung in two braids, and her flowery cotton nightgown fluttered in the frigid, early-morning breeze. In her left hand, she held a smoking deer rifle.

"Daniel!" she screamed. "Oh God, Daniel, no!"

She fell beside me as my arms gave out and I buried my drooling, gory face in the cool ice.

Gooley. Joe Gooley is still connected to the pump.

"Please, get up, Daniel! You're going to die if you lose too much blood!"

Using all of her strength and a hefty dose of adrenaline, she hoisted me up and wrapped my arm around her shoulders. Slowly, we trudged through the sharp, crusty snow, the blood from her scraped feet mixing with the red slobber dripping from my mouth.

I tried to speak, to tell her about Gooley. To tell her to drop me and save him. But only a gurgle escaped my lips, accompanied by a pink, frothy foam. It ran over my stubbly, white chin and down my neck and soaked into the collar of my undershirt.

"Don't speak, Daniel. I'm going to get you to a hospital. Everything is going to be okay!"

Please, Sandy. Drop me here. Let me die. It's not me who you should be worried about.

She threw me like a sack of potatoes across the back seat of her station wagon. Then everything went black. I remember nothing else of that day.

I've had a lot of days like that.

EPILOGUE

One charge of practicing without a medical license, four counts of extortion, five counts of aggravated kidnapping, and one charge of accessory to manslaughter. For all that, I was given a life sentence. The judge said "thirty-five years," but I won't make it that long. Prison is my final home. It is where I will die.

I received word that Jeremy, Lauren, Kevin, and Rebecka were revived successfully. But Joseph Gooley was found as lifeless and shriveled as a white raisin. All things considered, thirty-five years seemed light. Unfortunately, the accusations I leveled against the warden of an anonymous state prison were dismissed as the senseless ravings of a lunatic. I couldn't even provide a name.

The entire affair was an awful scandal—bigger than when I'd frozen myself. Even bigger and more horrible than when Gooley had been caught with those kids. Now both of us were together in the news for the salivating public's perverse enjoyment. And now I rot in the same penitentiary in Springfield where Gooley passed the time for nearly three decades. Maybe in the same cell.

I am no longer "Daniel Fassett." I am "Prisoner 70419." I am told when to eat, when to sleep, when to bathe, and when to speak. I'm told what I can read, who I can see, and where I can shit. I am stripped and searched weekly and dressed up in jumpsuits and chains almost daily.

Sandy was cleared of murder charges on the grounds of self-defense. Dr. Butcher had been on her property firing a deadly weapon in the direction of her house, after all. She, along with Mary and Nathaniel, moved out of state with my granddaughter to escape the media storm, and Ralphie will likely remain in Montana for the rest of his life.

And even still, I am waiting and dreaming. That, at least, has remained a constant in my life. Waiting to receive a letter from Elsie, a phone call from Mary, or a visit from Ralphie. In all my life, they are the simplest things I've ever held out hope for. But, as always, my dreams never come true. I may as well wish for an early release and the deed to the cottage in Florida. I may as well ask for all my years back, to live my life over the way I should have lived it the first time around. Ah, well.

At least I still have my blood.

ACKNOWLEDGMENTS

Thank you Sophie, Nathalia, Holly, Tom, Asher, and Amy Ellis; Barb and Jimmy Pappas; Nate Pollard; editors John K. Tiholiz and Marissa Graf; Dede Cummings and everyone at Green Writers Press; friends at JGHS; Phillis Mosher; Castle Freeman, Jr. and Bill Morgan; all booksellers and librarians; friends, family, and, most of all, readers.

ABOUT
THE
AUTHOR

JACKSON ELLIS is a writer and editor from Vermont who has also spent time living in Nevada and Montana. His short fiction has appeared in *The Vermont Literary Review, Sheepshead Review, Broken Pencil, The Birmingham Arts Journal, East Coast Literary Review, Midwest Literary Magazine,* and *The Journal of Microliterature.* He co-published VerbicideMagazine.com, which he founded as a print periodical in 1999. His debut, *Lords of St. Thomas,* received the 2017 Howard Frank Mosher First Novel Prize.